Not your typical summer camp

"Liliana Vera?"

In front of Lily stood a lanky counselor wearing a pine green Camp Atropos T-shirt, the name *Del* printed below the neckline.

"Are you Liliana?" Del asked. "I'm gathering Cabin Eight campers."

Lily glanced past Del to the flag circle, where four campers stood amid their luggage. "I'm Lily," she said.

"Great!" Del jerked his chin toward her duffel bag. "Need help with that?"

Lily shook her head, her wavy brown hair grazing her shoulders. "I got it," she said. Del looked skeptical, probably because Lily was hardly taller than the duffel was long. But Lily focused her thoughts at the bridge of her nose and, darting her eyes to the duffel, the bag rose—one inch, then five—off the ground. Lily took a step forward in the dirt, and the bag took a step with her.

"No need to ask what *your* Talent is," Del said, watching the bag drift forward. "Been a while since we had a Pinnacle here." Lily swelled with the smallest inkling of pride. "Welcome to Camp Atropos for Singular Talents, Liliana Vera. A haven for the most remarkable children in the world."

Other Books You May Enjoy

A Clatter of Jars

LISA GRAFF

PUFFIN BOOKS

PUFFIN BOOKS
An imprint of Penguin Random House LLC
375 Hudson Street
New York, New York 10014

First published in the United States of America by Philomel Books,
an imprint of Penguin Random House LLC, 2016
Published by Puffin Books, an imprint of Penguin Random House LLC, 2017

THE LIBRARY OF CONGRESS HAS CATALOGED THE PHILOMEL EDITION AS FOLLOWS:
Names: Graff, Lisa (Lisa Colleen), 1981– author.
Title: A clatter of jars / Lisa Graff.
Description: New York : Philomel Books, [2016]
Summary: "Children with magical Talents attend a summer camp,
where nothing is what it seems"—Provided by publisher.
Identifiers: LCCN 2015035538 | ISBN 9780399174995 (hardback)
Subjects: | CYAC: Fantasy. | Magic—Fiction. | Camps—Fiction. | BISAC: JUVENILE
FICTION / Social Issues / Friendship. | JUVENILE FICTION / Family / Siblings. |
JUVENILE FICTION / Fantasy & Magic.
Classification: LCC PZ7.G751577 Cl 2016 | DDC [Fic]—dc23

Puffin Books ISBN: 9780147516701

Printed in the United States of America.

1 3 5 7 9 10 8 6 4 2

Edited by Jill Santopolo. Design by Amy Wu.

Many thanks to Isaias Mercado for his help with the Spanish lyrics in this book.

To Aria,
a fizzy grape soda

Prologue

ON THE DARK WATERS OF LAKE ATROPOS, JUST OUTSIDE of Poughkeepsie, New York, there bobbed a single sailboat. At the boat's bow stood a black-haired pixie of a girl. Cadence, her name was. She and her parents were celebrating the one-year anniversary of her adoption.

The sky was offering a dazzling farewell to the sun—a fiery orange nearest the water, edging into watermelon pink farther up, then, at its height, a deep blackberry—and lily pads dotted the shore. Cady stared at the painted sky, passing an object between her hands.

It was a glass jar, sample-size, no larger than a Ping-Pong ball, with the words *Darlington Peanut Butter* embossed on the bottom. The jar was empty, save for the speck of light glowing at its center. Cady had seen the sight many times, and she never tired of it. The lower the sun dipped, the brighter the orb burned—dazzling yellow, like a firefly, smoldering purple at the extremities. The sphere always glowed brightest at the moment the sun set completely, then dulled to nothingness by morning.

When she heard her mother approach from the stern, Cady tucked the jar away.

"Toby and I were thinking of heading back to shore," her mother told her.

Toby was Cady's father—had always been her father, although they'd only recently discovered each other. Cady fit with Toby as though he were the matching left mitten to her right. Cady had known her mother, Jennifer, much longer, although they'd only recently become family. Cady fit with Jennifer as though she were the right mitten to Cady's left.

Somehow, though, Toby and Jennifer did not match each other, not in the slightest. Whether it was their stitching, or the dye of their yarn, Cady's parents did not make a pair. Toby didn't seem to mind so much, being unmatched. But Jennifer . . .

Sometimes Cady wondered if there wasn't another mitten out there somewhere for her mother. But whenever Cady broached the subject, Jennifer insisted she wasn't interested in mittens.

In the past year, Cady had gained more family than she'd ever dared dream of. A mother, a father, and two grandparents—a grandmother who spoke in music instead of words, and a thieving grandfather who'd left Cady a peanut butter factory, her new home. Most times, Cady felt like the luckiest girl in the world.

But sometimes, like when the sun blazed an orange-watermelon-blackberry trail across the lake, Cady dared dream for just a little bit more. An aunt, perhaps. Or a brother. A sister, even.

It might be awfully nice to have a sister.

"Two more minutes?" Cady asked her mother.

"Two more minutes," Jennifer agreed, then returned to the stern of the boat.

Alone once more, Cady took out her jar, examining it in the light of the setting sun. The glass glowed with possibility.

A Talent, that's what gave the jar its yellow-purple glow. A mysterious Talent stolen by Cady's grandfather. A Talent for acrobatics, perhaps, or for mending sweaters. It might allow Cady to translate Swahili, or train cats, or even turn raindrops into sparks of lightning. For a girl who just one year ago had lost all but a sliver of her own Talent, those were great possibilities indeed.

The only way to discover what lay inside the jar was to open it.

Cady studied the horizon, letting the jar and its glow of possibility dangle over the sailboat's edge. Then, unclasping her hand, she let the jar fall.

Plop!

The jar hit the water and sank swiftly down.

The things Cady dared dream of, she knew, couldn't be found in a jar.

Only two living creatures knew which Talent gave that jar its glow. The first was Cady's grandfather, Mason Darlington Burgess, who had Eked the Talent from a woman named Maevis Marvallous some thirty years previous.

The second was a man who knew what was inside most everything.

The woods of Camp Atropos for Fair Children, situated on the southernmost bank of the lake, were generally reserved for campers. The man in the gray suit was most certainly not a camper, and yet he stood watching the tide lap gently at the pebbly shore. He might have been forty, he might have been older—no one ever seemed able to tell for sure—and he was so large that his head had brushed several tree branches that were not used to being brushed. Bits of knotted rope peeked out from under his suit jacket, dancing with the summer breeze. Mason Darlington Burgess, the infamous Eker, had once tried to steal the man's Talent for knot-tying, trapping it in a jar, as he'd done with so many other Talents. But as Fate would have it, the Talent had not remained trapped.

At the man's foot squatted a frog, bright green on top and white at the throat, with bulby pads at the ends of his toes.

Hdup-hdup! went the frog.

———

"The lake should be nice and warm this summer," the man said. "Prime opportunity for swimming." Anyone who happened upon the scene would have sworn it was the frog the man was speaking to. "Might be warm for at least five summers to come."

Hdup-hdup! agreed the frog.

The sky continued to darken, the frog remained still but for the occasional billowing of his throat, and the man in the gray suit watched the water, wearing the sort of sideways grin that suggested he knew more about the world than he was letting on. When the last rays of light sank below the water, the man left the shore and cut through the thicket of trees. The frog followed. When they reached a sturdy log building at the center of the camp, the man in the gray suit started up the steps.

"We ought to let her know," he said.

Together, the man and the frog entered the lodge, passing beneath a moose head keeping guard above the doorway. An office was tucked just to the left of the lodge's entrance, with a plaque on the door that read CAMP DIRECTOR. The man in the gray suit knocked.

"Ah. My new bread vendor." The woman who tugged open the door had wild curly black hair, and creases around her mouth from years of frowning. She frowned now. "I thought we scheduled the delivery for tomorrow."

"It's awfully buggy down at the lake," the man in the gray

suit replied, which was no response at all. "Especially at sunset. Too much brush, I suppose. Ought to be cleared up."

The woman patted the pocket of her knitted sweater. "Is that a frog?" she asked, of the creature squatting in the doorway.

"Sunset," the man repeated. "Don't forget."

And then, without warning, the bright green frog with the white throat and the bulby pads at the ends of his toes leapt— *hdup-hdup!*—directly at the woman, landing on her shoulder.

Ignoring the camp director's squawk of surprise, the frog leapt again. The woman turned to follow the creature's path out the open window, but he was impossible to track in the dark night.

"Well, *that* was odd," the woman said. But when she spun back to the doorway, the man in the gray suit had disappeared as well.

As Fate would have it, the small glass jar that read *Darlington Peanut Butter* did not sink to the bottom of the lake entirely undisturbed. Anyone who happened upon the scene— although of course no one would ever happen upon such a scene, not at the bottom of a lake—would have noticed that on its way down, the jar struck a large black stone.

Just a titch.

Just enough.

The stone dislodged the jar's lid.

But, of course, no one saw.

Five Years Later . . .

Lily's Watermelon Limeade Float

a drink reminiscent of all the best birthday parties

FOR THE WATERMELON LIMEADE:
- 4 cups chopped watermelon, from half of one small watermelon
- 2 tbsp lime juice, from one lime
- 1/2 cup sugar
- 1 liter (4 cups) seltzer

FOR THE FLOAT:
- vanilla ice cream

1. In a blender or food processor, blend the watermelon, lime juice, sugar, and seltzer for just a few seconds, until smooth. Carefully pour through a wire-mesh strainer into a 2-quart pitcher. Discard the solids.

2. To serve, scoop ice cream into the bottom of a short glass. Pour the watermelon limeade over the top, and enjoy!

[Serves 8]

Lily

LILY STOOD OUTSIDE THE DOOR TO THE INFIRMARY, winding the length of swampy green yarn around her right thumb. In every corner of the woods, campers were squealing, laughing, making friends, and generally kicking up a lot of dust. But Lily was focused on that length of yarn.

"Liliana Vera?"

In front of Lily stood a lanky counselor wearing a pine green Camp Atropos T-shirt, the name *Del* printed below the neckline.

"Are you Liliana?" Del asked. "I'm gathering Cabin Eight campers."

Lily glanced past Del to the flag circle, where four campers stood amid their luggage. "I'm Lily," she said.

"Great!" Del jerked his chin toward her duffel bag. "Need help with that?"

Lily shook her head, her wavy brown hair grazing her shoulders. "I got it," she said. Del looked skeptical, probably because Lily was hardly taller than the duffel was long. But Lily focused her thoughts at the bridge of her nose and, darting her eyes to the duffel, the bag rose—one inch, then five—off the ground. Lily took a step forward in the dirt, and the bag took a step with her.

"No need to ask what *your* Talent is," Del said, watching the bag drift forward. "Been a while since we had a Pinnacle here." Lily swelled with the smallest inkling of pride. "Welcome to Camp Atropos for Singular Talents, Liliana Vera. A haven for the most remarkable children in the world." As they neared the flag circle, Del pointed to each of the four campers, rattling off names. "Miles, Renny, Chuck, and Ellie." Lily did a double take when Del named the last two. Chuck and Ellie were identical twin girls. "Your bunkmates for the next two weeks. Let's get you all to Cabin Eight, shall we?"

"Hi!" Ellie greeted Lily as they began their trek though the woods. Lily could tell the twins apart because, despite having identical faces and identical dark brown skin, Ellie had a headful of teeny braids pulled into a ponytail and was wearing pale blue sneakers, while Chuck's hair was styled into wavy cornrows, and she wore Kelly-green high-tops. "Do you like frogs?" Ellie asked. "Chuck and I can identify any species."

"Uh," Lily replied. "Cool."

That's when one of the boys, Miles, piped up. "Singular Talents are understood as feats beyond standard human abilities and/or the laws of physics," he said. His voice was flat, his gaze fixed on the dirt in front of him as he walked.

"Huh?" Ellie asked.

"I think what he means," said the other boy, Renny, "is that identifying frogs isn't a Singular Talent. Either that or he just likes showing off how much of that textbook he memorized."

Beside her sister, Chuck snorted. "Oh, man," she said. "They're on to us now, Ellie. I guess we'll have to leave and go to regular person camp."

Ellie poked her twin in the side. "Chuck, *please*," she said.

They were deep in the shadows of the trees when Renny joined step beside Lily. He was tall and skinny, with pasty white legs. "Is this your brother?" Renny asked, his nose buried in a small photo book. He flipped a page. "Cute kid."

"Hey!" Lily cried, realizing what Renny was holding. "Give me that!" Focusing her thoughts at the bridge of her nose, she tugged the photo book toward her through the air. With her concentration no longer upon it, her duffel thunked to the dirt. The front pocket had been zipped open.

Lily inspected the album for damage, wiping away a smudge from the photo of Max's fifth birthday party three years earlier. It was one of Lily's favorites. Her little brother was balancing a plate of chocolate cake on his pinkie, his other arm wrapped around Lily. Lily, meanwhile, was using her own Talent to push the cake toward Max's nose. It was the last birthday she and Max had celebrated before their mother remarried and their stepsister, Hannah, buzzed into their lives like a housefly. Hannah had to go and be born the same day as Max—same year and everything—so in every birthday photo after that, it was Hannah that Max had his arm around.

At least Hannah had been assigned to a different cabin for the two weeks of camp, Lily reminded herself, zipping the photo book back in its pocket. She hoisted the duffel to her shoulder, which immediately ached in protest.

"You should keep a better eye on your stuff," Renny said. And when Lily scowled, he didn't even have the decency to look sorry. Instead, he stretched out his arm, like he wanted to shake hands. "Renwick Fennelbridge," he told her. "You might have heard of me."

Despite herself, Lily was impressed. She'd studied the Fennelbridges last year in her Singular Education elective, and she found them fascinating. Every family member was Singular, with some of the most fantastical Talents ever recorded.

"Can you really read minds?" she asked.

That's when the other boy, Miles, piped up again. "Renwick Chester Ulysses Fennelbridge," he said, his eyes still fixed on the dirt. "Eleven years old as of his last birthday. The only living Scanner, according to *A Singular History.* Fun fact: Renwick Fennelbridge was once flown to Rome, Italy, to read the mind of the pope, but got food poisoning on the plane and had to go home."

"*Please* find a new fun fact, Miles," Renny grumbled.

"You really know your Talent history, huh?" Lily said to Miles. Singular Education had been Lily's favorite class last year. Her teacher had been so impressed with her report on Ekers and Coaxes that she'd had Lily read it during the opening ceremony of the Talent festival. "Do you know about Evrim Boz?"

Miles responded without hesitation. "Evrim Biber Boz. Born 1576, died 1602. Talent: Coax. Able to wheedle Talents from one person to another and back again, even transferring Talents into inanimate objects to create Artifacts. Fun fact: The Talent Library in Munich, Germany, has eight of Evrim Boz's Artifacts on display, including a cooking pot that makes anything boiled inside taste like lentil stew."

"Did you know that later in her life, Evrim Boz said she wished she'd never created any Artifacts at all?" Lily asked, scurrying to keep up with him. Unlike Ekers, who could only steal Talents, Coaxes could pass Talents on—either to other people or to objects. "Because once you make an Artifact, you can't get the Talent back out. Evrim Boz tried once, with a pair of scissors that she'd Coaxed a beard-trimming Talent into, and instead she accidentally replaced the beard-trimming with her brother's Talent for cartography." Lily had always had a particular interest in Artifacts and the people who used them. "Evrim Boz's brother never spoke to her after that."

Miles didn't even glance at Lily before continuing his recitation. "Maevis Marion Marvallous. Sixty-seven years old as of her last birthday. Talent: Mimic. Able to duplicate the Talent of any person she comes in contact with for approximately one year."

"Now you've set him off," Renny muttered. "When Miles gets started on Talent history, good luck getting him to stop."

"Fun fact," Miles went on. "Maevis Marvallous alleges that she lost her Talent over three decades ago, although scholars debate the claim."

Suddenly Lily noticed that Miles and Renny had the same sharp nose. Same auburn hair. Same pasty knees. Miles was a bit broader, but they were brothers, no question.

"I didn't know there were two Fennelbridge kids," Lily said. She was sure *A Singular History* had mentioned only one. "What's his Talent?"

Renny halted midstride to tug at the top of his right sock. "Make enough Fennelbridges, and one of them's bound to be Fair." He let out a sour laugh. "That's what our dad likes to say."

"If you ask me," Chuck chimed in, "there are two Fair kids in the Fennelbridge family."

"What do you mean by that?" Renny snapped.

"You obviously stink at reading minds," Chuck informed him. "I've been mentally threatening to pop you in the jaw for the past ten minutes, and you haven't flinched once."

Lily couldn't help it. She laughed.

Oblivious to the awkwardness behind him, Del pointed to a sturdy building hewn from logs. "There's the lodge," he called back. "Meals are served on the mess deck. All-camp slumber party's the second Friday of camp, and the Talent show's that Sunday, before your parents take you home."

At the mention of the Talent show, Lily's heart snagged her chest. Maybe there was still time to come up with a new act to perform with Max.

A lot could happen in two weeks.

"The lodge also houses the office of our camp director, Jo," Del continued. "She plays a mean harmonica."

Miles broke from his Talent history just long enough to tell the dirt, "I play a nice harmonica. I learned last year in music. Cassandra Colby Donovan. Born 1851, died 1900. Talent: Quest. Fun fact: Cassandra Donovan was the Needle-in-a-Haystack champion of Baxley, Georgia, for forty years running, until they retired the competition."

"Up ahead is the archery ring," Del went on. "There's the fire pit, where we hold our campfire each Friday. And if you squint, you can make out the lake through the trees."

At that, Miles stopped walking. "No water!" he squeaked.

Del offered Miles a friendly smile. "What's wrong with a little"—he spit into one hand and pressed his palms together before sprinkling miniature icicles in the dirt—"*water?*" He took in Miles's alarmed expression. "Not a fan of a classic Numbing Talent, huh?" Del cleared his throat. The ice-spit at his feet was already melting in the sun. "Uh . . . canoes are available every day after breakfast, and if you feel like swimming, Jo encourages you to grab your towel any time of day and hop right in the water."

"*No water!*"

Miles shrieked it that time. And he began flicking his fingers, too—*flick-flick-flick-flick-flick!*

Quick as lightning, Renny grabbed his brother's hand. "You guys sell Caramel Crème bars at the camp store, right?" Renny asked Del. Miles's fingers slowly ceased their flicking. "Miles loves Caramel Crème bars."

"I want a Caramel Crème bar," Miles said, pulling his hand free. If Lily hadn't witnessed the scene herself, she'd never have believed that Miles had been in a near panic thirty seconds earlier.

"Uh . . ." Del scratched a spot below his ear. "What was the question again?"

"Caramel Crème bars," Renny reminded him.

"Oh. Right."

As Del went over the store's hours, Lily wound the length of yarn around her thumb, watching Renny with his brother. Lily had tied the yarn around her thumb three weeks ago. Since then, the lime green strands had turned swampy, thinning and separating, and the skin underneath had grown raw from constant rubbing. It had stung for some time, like a blister—insistent, sharp, painful. But Lily hadn't untied it.

She tugged her duffel farther up her aching shoulder, her attention stolen by the music drifting through one of the lodge's windows. It was a song Lily was quite familiar with. This was an instrumental version, without lyrics, but Lily knew the words by heart.

> *Los golpes en la vida*
> *preparan nuestros corazones*
> *como el fuego forja al acero.*

Lily and Max's father had sung them the melancholy lullaby countless times, on nights when he wasn't traveling for work. When he sang the tune, the notes swept you up and cradled you, made you feel safe.

("Why do you always have to travel?" Lily had asked him last year, when he'd been in Prague instead of her school auditorium for the opening ceremony of the Talent festival. He'd responded as he always did. Not that it was his job—not that he *had* to be away so often, that he had no choice—but rather: "Oh,

Liria. Traveling helps ease my heartache." Which didn't explain why her father had begun his travels long before he and Lily's mother had been married.)

Lily let the words of the song sink in. Her father had translated the lyrics for her once, but she never felt she truly understood them in any language.

> *The blows of life*
> *prepare our hearts*
> *like fire forges iron.*

Summer camp, Lily thought, pulling herself from the music to rejoin the tour, didn't seem like a place for melancholy songs.

When they reached Cabin Eight, Del creaked open the door and let them inside.

"Cordelia Fabius Sibson," Miles said as he entered the cabin. "Eighty-two years old as of her last birthday. Talent: Scribe."

Lily wound the length of yarn around her right thumb, staring at the three bunks that lined the cabin walls.

Three bunks.

Six beds.

"Are we waiting for another camper?" Chuck asked Del. "There are six beds, and only five of us."

"The assignments for this cabin were a little odd," Del

admitted. "I don't know what Jo was thinking, but you don't question Jo. Anyway, you were supposed to have one more cabinmate, but at the last minute, he—"

Lily dropped her duffel with a heavy *thunk.* "I need to go to the infirmary," she said.

"You okay?" Del asked, stitching his eyebrows together.

"I have to go," Lily repeated. And she squeezed past him out the door, racing down the path. Kicking up dirt.

It should have been Max in that sixth bed. It should have been their summer together, while Hannah the housefly was far off in a different cabin, buzzing at someone else. But they weren't together, because three weeks ago, Max had gotten hurt.

Around and around went the length of yarn.

Lily was the one who'd hurt him.

Jo

JOLENE MALLORY DUG HER HAND DEEP INTO THE pocket of her knitted sweater, retrieving her harmonica. The instrument was well used and well loved, silver, scuffed, and slightly dented at one end.

Running her thumb over the harmonica's mouthpiece, Jo let her gaze settle on the smattering of sample-size glass jars that sat on her office shelves. Soon those shelves would be overflowing with hundreds of identical jars, carefully labeled and sorted. At the moment, however, there were a mere half dozen. Each jar was hardly larger than a Ping-Pong ball, with the words *Darlington Peanut Butter* embossed on the bottom. And to most people, they would have appeared empty.

Jolene Mallory was not most people.

Her gaze fixed upon the leftmost jar, Jo put the harmonica to her lips and, ignoring the sounds of the three hundred campers arriving for the first session of the summer, she began to play.

> *Los golpes en la vida*
> *preparan nuestros corazo—*

"You think you'd get sick of that song, after a while."

Jo swiveled around to face the man in the doorway, who was holding a familiar briefcase. "I thought I locked that door, Caleb," she growled.

Caleb studied his nails, as though thoroughly bored by the conversation already. "You did. You also sold me a Talent for lock-picking last week."

Jo drew a deep breath, which resulted in an accidental *waaaaah* from her harmonica. With the note, Jo saw a swirl of color around Caleb's scalp. Sunshine yellow, with streaks of puce.

Lock-picking, indeed.

"Shut the door," she told him.

"I brought someone along to meet you," Caleb replied. At his insistence, a boy, about five years old, stepped into the doorway. The child clung to Caleb's side.

"This isn't a day care," Jo said.

"Danny's my nephew. You'll like him." When Jo scowled, Caleb let out a truffly laugh. "Well, maybe *you* won't, but most people do. Only one thing." Caleb mussed the boy's hair. "Hasn't found his Talent yet."

Danny gazed up at Jo with big, wet eyes.

"I don't do party tricks," Jo informed them.

"No, of course not. Only business." Caleb examined the shelf along the wall, his eyes narrowed as though working through careful calculations. "How many jars is that you have to sell me today?" he asked. "Twenty?"

Jo flipped the harmonica end over end. The instrument was shiniest near the edges, where so many fingers had handled it. Her grandma Esther had bought the harmonica at an antique store in Istanbul over seventy years ago, from a fool who didn't realize its value. That and a gold pocket watch, similarly purchased, had been the heart of Grandma Esther's collection. Artifacts, they were called. Rare objects imbued with Talent.

"Twenty?" Jo asked, taking in the six tiny jars. "Have you gone blind? There are only—" When Caleb pulled the thick wad of bills from his pocket, Jo suddenly understood. "There are fifty at least."

Caleb snorted. "Looks more like thirty to me," he said, eyes on his cash.

Little Danny took it all in, shifting his attention from one adult to the other.

———

"There are forty-five jars on that shelf," Jo said firmly. "And not one fewer."

Caleb counted off the bills with the speed of a shrewd negotiator. "Forty-five jars." Jo took the money without bothering to count. Caleb was a crook, but he was no cheat.

Jo opened the top drawer of her desk and pulled out an envelope, tucking the cash inside. "Come in," she said. "Both of you. And shut the door."

With the door securely closed, Jo returned her harmonica to her lips. It didn't matter which song she chose—the magic was in the harmonica itself, not the notes it made. But Jo had her favorite tune. As she played, she heard the voice of the man made famous for singing it, the Talented singer they called El Picaflor. The Hummingbird.

> *Los golpes en la vida*
> *preparan nuestros corazones*
> *como el fuego forja al acero.*

Jo never knew quite what she'd see when she played Grandma Esther's harmonica. The colors—different every time, depending on the person she played for—rose with the notes, swirling in a mass of hues that only Jo could see. And somehow, when she was playing Grandma Esther's harmonica, Jo could interpret those colors. The surge of autumn shades with dots of

Mediterranean blue she saw when playing for her father, that was a Talent for calligraphy. The bright fireworks of copper and pink that danced above her mother, that was a Talent for plumbing. Catching lizards, growing tomatoes, interpreting dreams, parallel parking, caning chairs, telling lies—Jo had seen them all. Before Jo had discovered those first glowing jars at the edge of the lake, when Atropos had still been a camp for Fair children, playing her grandmother's harmonica had been Jo's greatest joy. Most people who called themselves Fair simply hadn't discovered their Talents yet, and Jo had the tool to change that. There was a thrill in it, but there was a worry, too. Jo felt it every time.

On rare occasion, when she played Grandma Esther's harmonica for someone new, Jolene Mallory saw no colors at all. And Jo knew precisely how unbearable it was to be one of the unlucky few who were truly Fair. These days, most people assumed that it was Jo who had the Talent and that the harmonica was merely the instrument she used to express it. Jo never bothered to correct them. The more mundane her Artifact was thought to be, the safer it was.

Jo was relieved when, with the first notes of El Picaflor's song, colors swam above Danny's head. Rose. Fuchsia. Geranium. Delicate strands, stretching for the sky. She pulled her harmonica to her chest.

"You have a Talent," she informed Danny—and the boy's

body relaxed, before she'd even finished the thought—"for cooking asparagus."

"*Asparagus?*" It was the first word Danny had uttered, and he uttered it loudly. "Uncle Caleb, she's wrong. I *hate* asparagus."

Caleb pulled a peppermint from his pocket and whipped it from its wrapper, stuffing the candy into Danny's mouth. "Jo's never wrong," he informed his nephew. "But don't worry. We'll buy you a better one."

Danny glared at Jo as he sucked on his candy. She ignored him. Jo was accustomed to the resentment that often came with the truth.

"I do have work to do," she said, pulling open her desk's middle drawer. She slid a roll of brown tape over her wrist, then tucked a black marker behind one ear, where it disguised itself in her wild dark curls. From the stack of colored bracelets, woven from embroidery thread, Jo plucked six.

"By all means," Caleb told her.

Jo made her way again to the shelf along the wall. With necessary speed, she—*whift!*—unscrewed the lid of each jar, slipping a single bracelet inside before sealing the container back tight. Then, with bracelets coiled safely at the bottoms of all six jars, Jo returned her harmonica to her lips.

There was, as always, a single Talent in each jar, sparkling and shining beneath the closed lid. Jo labeled all six with a precisely placed strip of tape, writing in her neat, blocky script.

WHISPER. That was a Talent for calming horses. QUICK. Speed-reading. DARK. Seeing through blackness. CLOTHES. Folding laundry. TONSILS. Performing tonsillectomies. Her stomach clenched with hope as she played, same as it always did with a batch of new jars. From the moment she'd plucked the first jar from the lake, glowing with possibility, Jo had hoped to discover a certain Singular Talent. But the right Talent hadn't found her yet.

Jo shifted her attention to the sixth and final jar, with its silver bracelet coiled at the bottom.

Los golpes en la vida
preparan nuestros—

Jo stopped.

She had never seen such colors before. For no reason Jo could explain, she was reminded of the man she'd seen canoeing in Lake Atropos the previous afternoon, wearing a three-piece gray suit. He'd looked so like the fellow she'd met five years ago, the man with the bits of knotted rope poking out from under his suit jacket, that she'd flubbed her bunk assignments, grouping a hodgepodge of boys and girls of all different ages into Cabin Eight. Jo hadn't witnessed the man leaping out of the canoe to take a dip in the lake, but perhaps he had.

"This one's not for sale," Jo told Caleb of the jar with the silver bracelet. She left the jar unlabeled, since she could think of no label for it.

"But I paid for all of them," Caleb argued.

Without a word, Jo opened her top desk drawer and returned a wad of bills. Then she sealed the envelope, thick with cash, to deposit in the bank that afternoon.

She tossed young Danny the jar with the red bracelet, labeled DARK. "That's the one you'll want," she told him. Then, her business resolved, Jo seated herself at her desk, and began to write a letter.

"How long does it take for the Talent to absorb into the bracelet, Uncle Caleb?" Danny asked, as Jo pulled out a sheet of stationery.

Caleb slipped the remaining labeled jars into the perfectly sized padded slots of his custom briefcase. Most of the slots remained empty, but he'd fill them easily at the next visit. "Talent bracelets aren't Artifacts," he replied, snapping shut the case. "They don't absorb the Talent, just carry it for you. A sort of"—he tapped his briefcase—"suitcase, if you will. Careful with that now, Danny. That's the real deal, not like those fake bracelets you get in gumball machines. You put that on, you'll be the most Talented kid in your kindergarten. No one will have to know you're also carrying around a Talent for"—Caleb lowered his voice—"*asparagus.*"

"The real deal," Danny repeated.

Dear Jenny, Jo wrote. She heard Caleb take one step through the office door, then stop.

"Run off to the car," Caleb told his nephew. "I'll meet you there."

Jo swiveled in her chair, leaving her thoughts—*I hope, as always, that my letter finds you well*—unfinished.

When he saw he had her attention, Caleb said, "Jo, you and I have been in business together, what, five years?" Jo set her pen down, already annoyed. "And I've always said your product is the finest in a very thin market."

"But . . . ?" Jo let her voice rumble, the first warnings of a gale.

"There's been talk among my buyers that your Talents have been . . . fading."

Jo turned back to her letter. "Caleb, if you're failing to inform your customers that those are Mimics"—she gestured to his briefcase—"then that's your headache." *You must already know what I'm going to ask you,* she wrote. "Mimics last one year. Everyone knows that."

"And yet somehow lately they've been fading faster. Jo, last summer I got complaints the Talents dwindled after only ten months. In the spring I heard five. I've been brushing it off as rumor. But yesterday one of my most trustworthy clients comes to me, says the Talents I sold him didn't even last two weeks."

"You picked that lock just fine, didn't you?" Jo replied. A ruse to stiff her on the next order, that's all this was. *Can't you find a way to forget what happened,* she wrote, *after all this time?*

———

"I'm trying to help you, Jo," Caleb insisted. "Maybe it's time to find a different source."

Jo pushed her chair from the desk and strode to the door, pulling it open wider. "Maybe it's time *you* found a different source."

Caleb sighed. "See you next week, Jo," he said.

Jo waited until Caleb had followed his nephew through the empty lodge, passing beneath the moose head keeping guard above the double doors. Then she finished her letter.

> *You know I would love to see you again, and*
> *finally meet little Cady.*
>
>

Your sister,

Jo

Jo folded the letter into thirds, then sealed it shut inside its envelope to give to Del for the afternoon mail run. Jo had sent her sister one letter every week for the past twenty years. Jenny had never once responded.

Most people might have figured, after countless unanswered letters, that it was best to give up. And five years ago, Jo was ready to. But then Fate had led her to those glowing jars, with the words *Darlington Peanut Butter* embossed on the bottom—the name of the very location where Jenny had taken up residence. And when Fate led you somewhere, Jo believed you'd better follow.

Jenny would forget, Jo told herself. One day, the right camper would arrive at Camp Atropos for Singular Talents, and Jenny would forget everything. In the meantime, Jo had work to do.

Her thoughts elsewhere, Jo plucked an envelope off her desk, folding it in half and sticking it in her back pocket for Del's mail run.

It was not the correct envelope.

Her thoughts elsewhere, Jo left the office.

She forgot to shut the door.

Renny

IT WAS A LONG WALK FROM CABIN EIGHT TO THE CAMP
store, and it was made much longer by Miles, who was going
about as slow as a two-legged toad.

"Grisiano Antonio Venerando," Miles said, as flat voiced as
ever. Renny did his best to tune him out. "Born 1916, died 1976."

As the camp store and its candy bars came into view, Renny
halted in the path, suddenly realizing that he'd left his spending
money back at their cabin.

(*"Talent: Recollector,"* Miles went on, oblivious. *"Able to
transplant memories from one mind to another."*)

Fifteen minutes back to Cabin Eight, and fifteen minutes
to return to the store. That was a whole lot of Talent history to
listen to.

("*Fun fact. There have been only three Recollectors in known history. Grisiano Antonio Venerando, Gertrude Maebelle Futch, and—*")

"Miles Fennelbridge!" came a voice from down the path. It was a woman with wild black curls, wearing a knit sweater over her Camp Atropos T-shirt. "Why, you're the spitting image of your father! And Renwick, too. I'm a lucky lady to have *two* Fennelbridges at my camp." There was an object in the woman's back pocket, Renny noticed. Flat and square, exactly the shape of a thick wallet. "I'm your camp director, Jo. But I'm assuming"—Jo winked at Renny—"you already knew that."

Renny *had* already known that, but not for the reason Jo probably thought. He'd recognized her from the camp brochure. Renny's parents had pored over that brochure endlessly, since they were considering Camp Atropos as an "investment opportunity." The Fennelbridges were constantly considering "investment opportunities." Renny could hardly take a bite of his breakfast cereal without his parents debating whether ChocoLoops was something they might want to throw money at.

Renny tugged at the top of his right sock. He was more than a little certain that his parents' habit of throwing money was the only reason Jo had agreed to let a Fair Fennelbridge into camp.

"Are you boys off for a swim?" Jo asked.

Beside him, Renny felt Miles go stiff. *"No water!"* he screeched, and he was already flicking his fingers—*flick-flick-flick-flick-flick! "No water!"*

"Miles isn't a big swimmer," Renny explained. Lowering his voice, he asked his brother, "Do you want to hold my hand, Miles?" He didn't wait for a response before clutching Miles's hand in his own. The flicking began to die down right away.

Most people—if they knew there were two Fennelbridge boys at all—tended to assume that Renny was oldest. Probably because most eleven-year-olds never asked their older brothers if they wanted to hold their hands. And most thirteen-year-olds probably never wanted to be asked. But the Fennelbridges, Renny's parents often reminded them, weren't most people.

Jo's mouth morphed into a frown. "Well," she said, "if you feel that strongly about the lake, Miles, I suppose you don't need to take a dip. But surely you'll go in, Renwick?"

Never one to miss an opportunity, Renny asked, "Can we go diving off that pier over there?"

As Jo turned around to see where he'd pointed, Renny's hands darted to her back pocket, snatching out the flat, square object. Jo didn't notice a thing. Renny was quick as a viper when he wanted to be.

"That's as a good a place as any to hop in," Jo replied. By the time she'd turned back, Renny already had his pilfered prize buried deep in his own pocket. Miles darted his eyes to the hidden loot, but Renny knew he wouldn't tell.

"Brother bond," Miles whispered, and Renny nodded. Miles didn't tell Renny's secrets, and Renny didn't tell Miles's.

"I'll be looking for you out in the water, Renwick," Jo said. "Be sure to go all the way under, toes to hair. That's the best way to soothe the sp—" Suddenly Jo put a hand on Renny's arm. "Where did you get that?"

For a moment, Renny's heart stopped beating. And then he saw where Jo was looking. Not at Renny's pocket, but rather at his right leg.

His sock had fallen down, just a little. Poking out from underneath was a bracelet, woven from blue and green embroidery thread.

"Uh." Renny bent down to tug at his sock. "Nowhere. It's nothing. Miles made it for me."

(*"Mason Darlington Burgess,"* Miles recited. *"Seventy-seven years old as of his last birthday. Talent: Eker. Able to absorb Talents from other people with a handshake."*)

Jo's face was dark, like a storm approaching. "Did you get that bracelet from my office, Renwick Fennelbridge?"

"What?" Renny said, truly baffled. "No. I told you, Miles made it for me."

"I didn't make the bracelet," Miles said, breaking out of his recitation. "Renny bought it from a gumball machine. It cost two quarters." Then Renny mouthed, *"Brother bond,"* and Miles clamped his mouth shut.

Renny watched Jo, unblinking, and she watched him. Each seemed to be waiting for the other to twitch first.

Finally, Jo said, "Why, Renwick, you *know* those things are a waste of money." Her face had brightened so quickly that Renny almost thought he'd imagined the darkness. "Besides, someone with a Talent as grand as Scanning has no need for a second one." She laughed. "Or did you already know I was going to say that, when you read my mind?"

Renny laughed, too. "Good one." He tugged at Miles's hand. "We gotta get Miles a candy bar."

"A Caramel Crème bar!" Miles shouted.

"Don't forget what I said, Renwick Fennelbridge," Jo called as they hurried away. "About the glorious dip in the lake. Toes to hair!"

"No water!" Miles shouted in reply. *"No water!"*

Most people who met Miles Patrick Francis Fennelbridge felt sorry for him. Everything seemed so difficult for him, all the time. Miles needed his chicken cut for him at meals, into even pieces. He needed his T-shirts folded, into precise squares. He was unbearably, inexplicably terrified of water. And heaven forbid you suggested he sleep on the top bunk in their cabin at camp. Top bunks, Miles had informed Renny loudly that morning, were NOT OKAY. So Renny got the top bunk, whether he wanted it or not, because helping Miles with difficult things stopped him from having one of his finger-flicking fits. But no matter how much Renny helped him, Miles was always going to be the Fennelbridge disappointment.

The truth was, Miles didn't seem to mind so much, being omitted from his parents' interviews. Standing alone in the doorway while a journalist posed the rest of the family for a photo. Knowing that their parents were coming to the camp Talent show to cheer only for Renny, and not for him. Somehow, the same kid who flicked and flailed at the very mention of water didn't seem bothered in the slightest that his parents wanted nothing to do with him.

Renny would have been bothered. He would've been bothered a *lot*.

Fortunately, neither brother needed to be bothered by much at all. Because Renny kept Miles's secrets, and Miles kept Renny's.

When they arrived at the camp store, Renny pulled out the object he'd swiped from Jo. He'd assumed it was a wallet. But it wasn't. It was an envelope.

"Want some peanut butter?" asked the counselor behind the storefront, whose thick ringlets were dyed neon pink. The name on her T-shirt said *Teagan*. "Best in the world." She showed them the large jar she'd been snacking from—*Darlington Peanut Butter*, the label read.

In the time it took Renny to glance at the jar and back, Teagan's pink ringlets had morphed into a sunshine-yellow bob.

"I want a Caramel Crème bar," Miles told her.

Renny weighed the envelope in his hand. Squeezed it. It didn't feel like any regular paper in there.

"You sure you don't want some peanut butter instead?" Teagan asked Miles, smearing some on a cracker. With every bite she took, her hair shifted again. *Crunch.* Short white spikes with purple tips. *Munch.* Long, straight, sleek, black. *Smack.* A polka-dot beehive. Teagan stuck her knife in the jar again, preparing a new cracker and handing it over.

His hands well below the height of the counter, Renny ripped the envelope open and peeked inside.

"*Whoa,*" he breathed.

Cash. Loads and loads of cash.

"Right?" Teagan said, as Miles chewed his cracker. "Isn't that the best peanut butter you ever ate?"

"Yes," Miles replied, still chewing. "I want a Caramel Crème bar."

Teagan laughed. "One dollar," she said.

Miles turned to Renny, who plucked a single bill from the envelope and handed it to his brother. Then he plopped the envelope, with the rest of the cash still inside, on the counter. "I found this in the dirt," he lied. "I think it might belong to the camp director."

Teagan took the envelope, and when she saw its contents, her hair flushed cardinal red. "That was very honest of you," she told him.

"I'm a very honest kid."

"I want a Caramel Crème bar," Miles reminded them.

"There's a case in the back," Teagan told him. *Crunch.* Her hair morphed again, chocolate-frosting brown. She lifted up the counter to let Miles inside. "You go grab one. I can't leave my post."

Miles made a beeline for the candy bars.

"You know they're going to stop making those candy bars, right?" Teagan told Renny, as Miles searched. "I heard it on the news last week. Shutting down production sometime this year." As Renny was contemplating the epic fit Miles would have if he heard *that* news, Teagan's hair morphed into pointy peach peaks. "You're that Fennelbridge kid, aren't you?" she said. *Munch.* Springy dolphin gray curls. "The kid who reads minds." *Smack.* Tangerine waves, down to her waist. Teagan pulled a pack of playing cards from the display on the wall, and ripped off the plastic, plucking out a card at random. "What card am I holding?"

Renny tugged at the top of his right sock. "Miles?" he called.

"He's fine," Teagan said, waving a hand toward the back of the shop. "Come on, read my mind."

If you made enough Fennelbridges, one of them was bound to be Fair. That's what their father liked to say.

"Just one card," Teagan urged.

"Found it!" Miles announced, heading to the counter with his candy bar. He stood just behind Teagan, at her elbow. "I need to pay now."

Teagan was still holding up that playing card. "Here, I'll concentrate on it," she told Renny. *Smack.* Her hair wove itself into a blue French braid. "Really focus. Does that help?"

"Miles is going to freak out if you don't let him pay," Renny told her. And then, when he was certain Teagan was focused on her card, Renny mouthed two words to Miles.

"Brother bond."

Flick-flick-flick-flick-flick! Miles began to flick his fingers like there was something sticky on the ends of them he was trying to shake off.

The seven of clubs.

"Seven of clubs," Renny told Teagan, as the image wiggled its way into his mind. He reached across the counter to still Miles's flicking fingers.

"What are you talking about?" Teagan asked, scratching below one ear. Even her hair looked bewildered.

"The card?" Renny reminded her. "You asked me to tell you what it was. And I said the seven of clubs."

Teagan looked at the card in her hands, and as soon as she did, her hair suddenly rose on her scalp, bright sparks of gold. "*Wow.* I'm going to tell everyone I got my mind read by *the*

Renwick Fennelbridge!" She tossed the playing card in his direction, and Renny caught it.

The seven of clubs.

Behind the counter, Miles was still holding his dollar. "I'm done helping now, and I want to eat my Caramel Crème bar," he said. When Teagan kept her gaze on Renny, Miles immediately shifted into a fit. "I can't *eat* it till I *pay*!" And he was flicking his fingers again—*flick-flick-flick-flick-flick!*

"That's enough now," Renny whispered, clutching his brother's hand once more. He gave the dollar to Teagan, who rang up the sale on the register.

As they made their way back to Cabin Eight, Renny glanced at Miles, who was munching away contentedly. "Thanks," Renny told him, when there was no one to hear but the squirrels. "For helping me back there."

"Miles Patrick Francis Fennelbridge," Miles said to the dirt. And Renny didn't bother to stop him, because there was no one to hear but the squirrels. "Talent: Recollector. Able to transplant memories from one mind to another. Fun fact: Only two people know about Miles Fennelbridge's Talent, and they have a brother bond."

Renny paused midstride to tug at the top of his right sock, which hid his blue and green Talent bracelet. His deepest, darkest secret.

There was one disappointment in the Fennelbridge family, and it wasn't Miles.

———

Miles Patrick Francis Fennelbridge, the unknown Recollector, had tugged many memories from many minds in his thirteen years, some purposefully, most not. The majority he flicked away without direction, allowing Fate to guide them. Not five minutes earlier, he'd tugged a memory completely without trying, from someone standing in the camp director's office.

As Fate would have it, that someone was a cabinmate of his.

Chuck

AS SHE STOOD JUST INSIDE THE DOOR OF CABIN EIGHT, clenching and unclenching her right hand, Chuck was painfully aware of her sister standing beside her, breathing the same air, waiting for her to make up her mind.

There were two empty bunks in Cabin Eight, which meant four empty beds. Only Miles and Renny had chosen sleeping spots so far. Four empty beds, and two girls, standing in the corner, staring at the floor. It shouldn't have been difficult for Chuck and Ellie to decide where they wanted to sleep. But it was.

"There's a frog outside the cabin," Ellie said, kicking at the floor with the toe of her pale-blue sneaker. "It's not native to this area, which is weird." She paused, as though waiting for Chuck to say something. Chuck did not. "You want to see it?" Ellie stretched out her hand, her left to Chuck's right.

Despite herself, Chuck took her sister's hand. And she could feel it, as soon as they touched—the icy spark that passed between them, like ice cream on a hot day. With the chill that crawled up her arm, into her chest, came the Talent.

Hdup-hdup! went the frog outside.

It was a white-lipped tree frog, Chuck could tell that now. Male. Juvenile. Bright green on top and white at the throat, with bulby pads at the ends of his toes. Chuck knew all of that without even seeing the creature. Chuck knew, too, that the frog was squatting directly outside the door of their cabin, puffing his froggy throat as though waiting for something spectacular to happen.

"We could start practicing our act for the Talent show after we unpack," Ellie said. "I have some really good ideas. I was thinking first I'll tell the frogs to hop to one side of the stage, and then you—"

Chuck pulled her hand away from Ellie's, only to offer it to her sister immediately afterward, palm up. "Stop pretending you can talk to frogs," she said. There was no way Chuck would stand on the lodge stage in front of three hundred campers and their parents, and do anything having to do with frogs. She gripped Ellie's hand tight, passing the Talent back. It always felt different going the other way—warm instead of cold. Ellie had told her once that when she got the Talent, it felt like hot cocoa, working its way into her heart.

"You should pick a bed already," Chuck said, letting her arm drop to her side.

"*You* pick."

If Chuck picked a bed first, then the second she did—the very *second*—Ellie would plop her stuff down on that same bunk, and that would be it. They'd be stuck together for two long weeks. Sharing a bunk, just like they shared everything else—a face, a room, a Talent. So Chuck was waiting for Ellie to pick first, so she could choose a bed on the *other* bunk.

Ellie, clearly, was waiting for Chuck.

They were still standing in the doorway when Del popped his head into the cabin ten minutes later. "Nice shoes, Frog Twin!" he greeted Chuck, noticing her Kelly-green high-tops.

Chuck let out a growl. When she'd begged her parents for those shoes last week, she'd thought they were the most unique ones in the store. Somehow it hadn't occurred to her till later that bright green shoes would only make her look more froggy. She dumped her duffel on the floor, wrenching the zipper open. She was sure she'd stuffed a pair of ratty water shoes in there somewhere.

"Del?" Ellie said as Chuck tore through her bag. "At the slumber party, everyone sleeps next to their cabinmates, right? And they sit together at meals, too? And at the campfire, and arts and crafts, and—"

Chuck shot to her feet. She'd have time to change her shoes later. At the moment, there were more urgent matters to attend to.

"Where are you going?" Ellie shouted as Chuck darted out the door.

"Don't follow me!" Chuck called over her shoulder. She clenched and unclenched her right hand as she raced down the dirt path.

Charlotte and Eleanor Holloway had discovered their Talent when they were four, on the afternoon of their Adoption Day party at Miss Mallory's Home for Lost Girls. Everyone had taken a break from games and cake (a chocolate-hazelnut ice-box cake for Chuck and a strawberry layer cake for Ellie) to stroll to the duck pond. And while their new parents were tearing up stale bread loaves not far away, Ellie had made an unusual announcement.

"Mink frogs!" she'd shouted. "Six of them, right there. Four boys and two girls."

Chuck had peered down into the pond, at the thick patch of lily pads where Ellie was pointing. At four, Chuck had never heard of mink frogs, but sure enough, she spotted one, poking his sleepy face out of the water. After a bit of a search, she spied another. Bright nose and a dark body, with brown splotches all over. Several minutes later, she'd found three more. "There's only five frogs," Chuck corrected her sister. "Not six."

Which was exactly the moment when the sixth frog leapt from the water and landed at Ellie's feet.

"Six," Ellie told her. "And there's a Fowler's toad in the bushes."

Four-year-old Chuck had been impressed. "Ellie!" she'd squealed, squeezing her sister's left hand with her right one, and wishing she felt half as spectacular as her twin clearly was. The grip was chilly, Chuck remembered. "You're *Talented!*" And then Chuck had let go of her sister's hand to point to a brown speck in a tree above them. "What's that one?"

To which Ellie, surprisingly, had not had a response. "I don't know," she'd admitted.

"You don't?" Chuck had asked. It was a spring peeper; Chuck was certain of it. She took Ellie's hand again, to help her remember how spectacular she was. This time the grip was warm.

"Spring peeper!" Ellie cried suddenly. "And a Northern leopard frog, in the bush!" The spotted creature raised himself on his front arms, puffing his throat silently, as though begging the twins not to reveal his hiding spot.

That's how Chuck and Ellie Holloway had discovered they shared a Talent. Only one sister could use it at a time, but together they had the most extraordinary ability to identify frogs. It was unusual, Chuck knew, to share a Talent. She'd never heard of two other people who had done it before—which was why, she suspected, they'd been allowed to attend Camp Atropos. Renny had been right earlier, about identifying frogs not being a Singular Talent. Chuck didn't mind not being Singular. But she'd give anything to be unique.

For years, it had been fun, sharing a Talent. But lately Chuck was beginning to get frog fatigue. Lately she'd begun wondering—with a sour sort of guilt in her stomach—how her life might have been different if Miss Mallory had matched her with another family, one that didn't have Ellie in it. Most times, Chuck felt her family was perfect. No complaints. But every once in a while, like when Ellie grabbed for her hand over and over and *over*, Chuck wondered if maybe she was meant for something else. If Chuck hadn't spent her whole life glued to her sister's side, how unique might she be?

Hdup-hdup!

Chuck stopped walking and turned slowly. There, squatting behind her on the path, was the white-lipped tree frog. He swelled his throat, the skin growing thin and translucent as it filled with air. And then he let out his call—remarkably loud for such a small creature.

Hdup-hdup! went the frog.

Chuck blinked at him. "Did Ellie tell you to follow—?" she began. And then she realized she was talking to a *frog*. She spun on her heel and started for the lodge again.

The frog hopped up the steps behind her. He seemed to know his way around.

The door to the camp director's office was open, so Chuck figured it was okay to wait inside. Out the window, past the camp store where Renny and Miles were buying candy bars, Chuck made out the lake, sparkling in the sunshine. She'd go for a swim, she decided, after Jo assigned her to a new cabin. Swimming always made Chuck feel like the mess of the world was far, far away.

Hdup-hdup! went the frog from the doorway. And then, his froggy legs splayed out behind him, he leapt straight for her. Chuck let out a squawk of surprise, but the creature hadn't aimed for her shoulder as she'd supposed. Instead, the frog landed—*thwop!*—on the shelf behind her. He puffed out his throat, watching her. *Hdup-hdup!*

Chuck peered at the object the frog had planted himself in front of. A small glass jar, empty except for a thin bracelet woven from silver embroidery thread. Chuck picked up the jar to examine it.

"What are you doing?" boomed a voice from the door.

Chuck didn't mean to. She really didn't.

Chuck dropped the jar.

The glass broke, shards scattering across the toes of Chuck's Kelly-green high-tops, the bracelet plunking itself among the laces. And in that moment, the white-lipped tree frog leapt again, this time landing at Chuck's feet. Squatting on his four froggy legs, he stretched apart his white lips—wide, wider, widest—and shot out his long pink tongue. And before Chuck could so much as blink, the frog had swallowed the bracelet. Gulped it completely down.

There was a horrified screech. The woman in the doorway, Chuck saw now, with the wild black curls, was the camp director, Jo. And she did not look pleased.

Jo dropped to the floor, knees in the glass, grabbing for the frog. But the creature escaped, leaping at Chuck again. Before she even realized she'd caught him, the frog had settled onto Chuck's palm.

Through the thin skin of the frog's white throat, Chuck could see that woven silver bracelet. "Why'd you do *that*?" Chuck whispered at him. As if in response, the frog puffed out his throat.

The silver bracelet shifted inside the frog.

One twist.

Puff.

Two twists.

Puff.

Around and around and around and around.

Puff puff puff puff.

"That frog," Jo said, rising to her feet, "stole my Talent." Her voice was a terrifying rumble.

"Talent?" Chuck asked.

At that, the frog—*hdup-hdup!*—spit out the bracelet into Chuck's open hand and hopped right out the window.

Chuck plucked up the bracelet with two fingertips. Wet and slimy, it had been tied into the most intricate knot she'd ever seen. Quirky and complicated and beautiful.

And as unforgettable as the entire scene was, in that instant ("I want to eat my Caramel Crème bar," came a voice from outside. "I can't *eat* it till I *pay!*") . . .

Chuck forgot it.

"This is neat," Chuck said, examining the knot between her fingertips. She looked up at the curly-haired woman. Jo, she thought her name was. Their camp director. Chuck scratched at an itch below her ear. "Did you make it?"

Jo narrowed her eyes at Chuck. "I don't think you're very funny, little girl."

Chuck scratched harder. "I wasn't trying to be funny," she said. She shook her head, trying to remember why she'd come. "I want to change cabins," she said at last.

"No reassignments," Jo snapped. She still had her eyes narrowed. "You're Charlotte, right? Chuck?" Chuck nodded. "I think it's best if you go now, Chuck."

"But—"

"Good-bye, Chuck."

The itch persisted, just below Chuck's ear, as she passed

beneath the moose head keeping guard above the lodge's double doors. She slipped the curious silver knot into her pocket and looked down the path to the lake, sparkling in the afternoon sun. A good swim, she figured, ought to clear her head.

Memory is a curious thing. Some details stick in our minds like peanut butter on crackers, and refuse to budge, as much as we might wish they would. Other memories—heavy ones sometimes, ones that seem unbudgeable—can be plucked right out when we least expect it. Lost memories leave remnants, of course, flavors that linger in the mind, but it's difficult to taste things when you don't know they're there.

All memories have a flavor, although not everyone can taste them. Chuck's memory, of the Talent bracelet and the frog and the silver knot, tasted of crisp peaches. And it was currently whistling its way down the dirt path of Camp Atropos, flitting this way and that in the wind, searching for a new mind to settle into.

Lily

FOCUSING HER THOUGHTS AT THE BRIDGE OF HER NOSE, Lily tugged open the door to the infirmary.

"Didn't expect to see you so soon," Nurse Bonnie greeted her. "Max is just settling in." She gestured toward the small room behind the curtain where the sick beds were.

When Max had first broken his leg three weeks ago, the doctor had assured their parents that two weeks of camp would be fine. Lily wondered if that doctor had ever been to camp. With an enormous cast covering his right leg, toe to thigh, Max could hardly do anything. He couldn't participate in cabin canoe races or Color War (Max and Lily would've *trounced* Hannah's cabin, for sure), and he had to sleep in the infirmary, in one of the beds reserved for campers who got sick in the middle of the night. It wasn't exactly what Lily had imagined when they'd signed up together.

"How are you feeling?" Lily asked, pushing through the curtain to find her brother propped up in bed. His crutches were perfectly balanced before a chest of drawers, without even leaning. As a Calibrate, Max could stabilize any object, from the most teetering tower of blocks to his own body, balanced on his head, his elbow, anything. Well, he *used* to be able to do all that. Since the accident, some of it was more difficult.

"My leg itches," he told Lily.

"You need more pillows?" Lily already had one in the air, focusing her thoughts, when Max shook his head. She let it fall back to the bed. "You really don't remember it?" she asked for the thousandth time. "The accident?" Around and around went the length of yarn.

"It's like I told that doctor," Max said. "I must've bonked my head too hard. Too bad you weren't there to help me."

"Yeah." Around and around and around. "Too bad."

Ever since they'd signed up for Camp Atropos, Lily had known that they'd need a killer act for the Talent show. It was the last thing they'd get to do before heading home, and everyone's parents would be in the audience. Their father would be there. He'd rearranged his schedule and everything. So when, while inspecting a photo in the Camp Atropos brochure of a girl breathing fire during last year's Talent show, Lily had spotted the bookshelf beside the lodge stage, she knew she'd been walloped with a fantastic idea.

For their act, Max would balance himself upside down on one finger, atop a teetering stack of books, and every time he shouted *"More!"* Lily would focus her thoughts at the bridge of her nose and tug another book off the bookcase. Then she'd shift her concentration back to her brother, and—*focused, focused*—lift up the entire stack of books with Max on top, sliding the new book underneath. Max had agreed to the idea right away. Of course he had. It would be phenomenal. Just the two of them, no Hannah.

Phenomenal.

Maybe Lily hadn't been concentrating enough on the books, during their first practice in the living room. Maybe she'd been concentrating a little too much on how pouty Hannah would look when her birthday buddy stole the show with Lily and not her. Because when Max was busy balancing, high up in the air, shouting *"More!"* Lily tugged a little too hard on the bookcase.

The books toppled first—*Whunk! Whunk! Whunk! Whunk!*— landing on Max in a horrible heap. Lily was so startled that she couldn't refocus. Before she realized what was happening, the bookcase was toppling, too. The entire heavy wooden structure landed—*thu-WHUNK!*—on top of Max's leg. And Max just lay there, eyes closed. Leg bent at a bad angle.

Lily screamed for her mom and Steve in the backyard, and they raced in right away. Lily saw them.

She saw Hannah racing, too.

What Lily did next, it was enough to make her stomach twist inside of her, like that length of yarn around her thumb, every time she remembered.

When she spied Hannah—she didn't know why, she just *did* it—Lily focused her thoughts behind the bridge of her nose, and she lifted the bookcase into the air, pushing it back against the wall, settled into its divots in the carpet. The books she left, scattered across the floor, but the bookcase she'd returned.

"I don't know what happened," she told everyone. Hannah was hunched over Max, yanking books off him like he was her brother, instead of her stepbrother. "I didn't see it." The words tasted as bitter as a cup of her father's coffee, but still Lily pushed them out. "I was getting some water." If Max ever learned the truth, he would never like Lily best. "He must've fallen over."

Lily had tied the lime green bow around her thumb that evening, so that even if no one else knew the truth, she would always remember.

She was fluffing another pillow for Max when she heard her least-favorite voice behind her.

"Hi, Max! I brought you something." Hannah stepped through the gap in the curtains, holding a glass of red juice.

Her blond hair, perfectly straight and incredibly long, swished past her waist. "I would've brought you a drink, too, Lily, but I didn't know you'd be here."

Lily rolled her eyes at that, all the way to one side and back again. The Talent Hannah had been born with, she would tell you (and *tell* you, and *tell* you), was for tasting the flavors of her memories—good ones, bad ones, scary ones. But about seven years ago, when she'd been a baby, Hannah's mother had taken her to a cake-baking competition in New York City, and the most curious thing had happened. One of the contestants—a girl, just about as old then as Lily was now, with a remarkable Talent for knowing the perfect cake to bake for anyone she met—had had her Talent stolen by an Eker, right in the middle of the bakeoff. The Talent had escaped, flooded the air that filled the room. And everyone who attended the competition had absorbed a tiny bit of it. The smallest of slivers.

Everyone, including Hannah.

With that sliver of new Talent, Hannah's memory-tasting had morphed into something different. Now she could bring out the flavor of other people's memories, too, by making one of her special concoctions. Hannah served drinks to practically everyone she met, whether they asked for them or not—juices, punches, smoothies, teas. Whoever drank one of Hannah's beverages could recall memories in vivid, sharp detail. Lily had tasted a few before, mostly by accident, and the clarity of the memories was, she hated to admit it, rather incredible.

"It's a strawberry basil juice bomb," Hannah told Max. "Wait till you taste it."

Max sucked down half the drink in one gulp, eyes closed. "First day I discovered my Talent," he said, popping his eyes open. "Thanks, Hannah."

Their stepsister plopped herself down on the edge of Max's bed, far too close to his injured leg. "I figured out what I'm going to do for the Talent show," she said. Not that anyone had asked. "I'm going to make a punch for the whole camp and serve it while everyone's performing. It's going to have memories from every single camper. Chef Sheldon said I could practice in the kitchen during free swim."

"Cool," Max said, taking another glug of his juice.

"Free swim sounds way better," Lily muttered.

"Wanna help me?" Hannah asked Max. "You can help, too, Lily."

"Sure," Max said, slapping his empty glass on the chest of drawers. "Sounds fun."

Lily sputtered at that, sending Max's crutches crashing to the floor. "You can't help Hannah," she told her brother. "You're doing an act with me." What would their father think if he rearranged his whole schedule and then all he saw was Max serving stupid punch with stupid Hannah?

Max frowned at her. "I can't balance upside down with my cast," he said. "I tried, and I can't." He turned back to Hannah. "Your idea sounds good."

"It does *not* sound good," Lily argued. She did her best to focus her thoughts and set Max's crutches upright again, but only managed to shoot them under the bed. "I already came up with a new act for us, just you and me."

"You did?" Hannah asked.

"You did?" Max said.

"Yeah," Lily replied. Around and around went the length of yarn. "I just have to work on a few more details, and I'll tell you all about it."

Max thought that over, sticking one finger underneath the ridge of his cast to scratch his leg. "I guess I could wait a few days to decide what to do," he said. "But I think we're supposed to start practicing soon."

"Don't worry," Lily said. "Our act's going to be *amazing*. Way better than punch."

As she made her way back to Cabin Eight, Lily wound the length of swampy yarn around her thumb, grumbling to herself. How was she supposed to come up with a brand-new act in only a few—

Peaches.

Lily stopped walking. There was the most curious feeling, like an itch in her mind. Something wiggling its way in. A memory.

A memory that tasted of crisp peaches.

She had broken a jar, she remembered. Lily scratched the itch harder. The glass had shattered across the toes of her Kelly-green high-tops. And there'd been a frog, and a silver knot . . .

Scratch scratch scratch.

There had been a bracelet in that jar. Lily remembered. A bracelet that stored a Talent. *Scratch scratch scratch.*

If Jo had one Talent in her office, then she might have more.

If Max had a different Talent, then it would be easy to create a new act.

The itch completely scratched, Lily spun on her heel and headed toward the lodge.

Jo's Blackberry Sage Iced Tea

a drink reminiscent of summer evenings on family porches

FOR THE TEA:
- approximately 7 cups water, divided
- 2 cups (12 oz) fresh or thawed frozen blackberries
- 2 tbsp sugar
- 4 black tea bags
- 8 fresh sage leaves

1. In a medium pot, bring 4 cups of the water to a boil.

2. Meanwhile, combine the blackberries and sugar in a medium bowl. Mash well with a fork.

3. When the water has reached a boil, remove it from the heat. Add the blackberry mixture, tea bags, and sage leaves. Cover and let sit 20 minutes.

4. Remove the tea bags from the pot and discard them. Carefully pour the tea through a wire-mesh strainer into a 2-quart pitcher, then discard the solids.

5. Add additional cold water (approximately 3 cups) to fill the pitcher. Stir the tea with a wooden spoon, and chill it in the refrigerator, about 1 hour. Serve over ice.

[Serves 6]

Jo

JO SWEPT THE SHARDS OF BROKEN GLASS INTO THE
dustbin, her insides boiling with each new *clank!*

That girl Chuck knew about her Talent bracelets. Which
meant that soon there would be questions. Phone calls from
parents. Trouble, and lots of it.

Jo patted the pocket of her knitted sweater, where she kept
Grandma Esther's harmonica. Some people, she knew, were
skittish about the buying and selling of Talents. But Jo found it
perfectly natural. If you didn't like your hair, you could dye it.
Cut it. Have it braided, permed, relaxed, shaved off completely.
So why not change your Talent, if you had the inclination?

Jolene Mallory understood more than most people about

Talent, and the lack of it, and how either could define you. Jo had grown up Fair. So had her older sister, and so had the boy next door. Jenny and Juan, both six years older, would pull little Jo around the backyard in their wagon, and climb trees with her, and tell her wild stories. As they grew older, the trio found wilder adventures, getting lost in museums, diving to the darkest depths of the coldest lake. All three of them were Fair—a rarity in a world of Talented people—and they formed a tight-knit club, making plans for their future. Three houses, side by side by side. Gardens out front they all helped tend to.

When Jenny and Juan fell in love, Jo was thrilled. When they got engaged, she was overjoyed.

And then Grandma Esther had died.

In her will, Grandma Esther had left Jo, then thirteen, her harmonica. She'd left Jenny, nineteen, her gold pocket watch. *For my two beloved granddaughters*, she'd written. *So they each may know a Talent.* The harmonica and the pocket watch were Grandma Esther's two most precious possessions, from a lifetime of collecting. Everyone knew that. But no one understood what they truly were until Jo put the harmonica to her lips.

Gold and tangerine and walnut and sunshine. Those were the colors Jo saw when she played the harmonica. And she was playing for *Jenny*.

"You're Talented," Jo had told her sister, pulling the harmonica—an *Artifact*—from her mouth. "Jenny, you're very, very Talented." Jennifer Mallory, it turned out, had a Talent for matching orphans with the perfect adoptive parents. As soon as Jo had seen the colors, she'd known.

And she'd known, almost immediately after, that she herself had no Talent at all. Not without the harmonica.

"Wind the pocket watch," Jo had urged Jenny. In order to reap the benefits of an Artifact, a person needed to use it, but even without winding its gears, Jo had seen the colors swirling around the watch when she played—chartreuse and fern, sea foam and pickle. It was a gorgeous Talent, mesmerizing. A Talent for singing.

But Jenny merely held the watch in her hand, studying its gears beneath the glass. "Maybe it's best to stick with the Talents we're born with," she'd replied—which, Jo would later decide, was easy enough to say when you'd been born with *something*. And then Jenny had snapped the watch shut.

Jo did not shut away her harmonica. She played it for nearly everyone she met. She played it for Juan—who, she discovered, was completely Fair, just as she was. But unlike Jo, he didn't seem to mind so much. He had Jenny, he said, and that was enough. Asking for more would be greedy.

As the wedding drew nearer, Jenny and Juan made more plans for their future. Once they were married, it was decided, they would open an orphanage—Jenny and Juan's Home for Lost Children. Jenny would match orphans with their lucky parents, and Juan would run the place, tending the garden, fixing broken steps. For the first time, Jo realized, their plans did not include her. She watched the calendar, her stomach twisting inside her, as the date she would lose her sister loomed ever nearer.

So Jo, thirteen and fearing the future, began a campaign to stop it from coming.

"Do you ever worry . . . ?" she'd said to Juan one night, when they were sipping blackberry iced tea on the porch swing. Jenny was inside being fitted for her wedding dress. "Do you ever worry that Jenny might get . . . ?" Jo trailed off, darting her eyes to her lap, as though consumed by words unsaid.

"Might get what?" Juan asked, taking a sip of his tea.

"Might get . . . bored," Jo finished, her voice thick with hesitation. "I mean, because she has such an incredible Talent, and you . . . It's just that, since she's *so* Talented, maybe she'd want . . ." She let her gaze drift to the thick of the woods. "You don't ever feel bad without a Talent?"

"Oh, Joley." Juan slugged Jo in the shoulder, the way a big brother slugs a little sister. "I don't need Talent to be happy." He took another long sip of his tea. And then, just when Jo's heart had begun to sink, he looked up. "Did Jenny say something to you?" he asked.

"Hmm?" Jo shook her head quickly. Too quickly. "Oh. Oh, no. She didn't say anything. I promise. I was just thinking."

But she could tell that a thought had wiggled its way into Juan's brain. And when thoughts wiggle their way in, sometimes it can be very difficult for them to wiggle out again. Sometimes, after months of wiggling, after a dozen more similar thoughts, if a little sister happened to leave out a gold pocket watch where her soon-to-be-brother-in-law might find it, you couldn't entirely say that it was her fault if he decided to wind it.

The Talent was even more mesmerizing than Jo had anticipated. As soon as Juan twisted the watch key and set the gears in motion, he was singing. Full-voiced and gorgeous.

> *Los golpes en la vida*
> *preparan nuestros corazones*
> *como el fuego forja al acero.*

The postman stopped his rounds to come listen. The town barber left his post to find the source of the sound. Children ceased their jump-roping. Even the squirrels seemed mesmerized.

"Remarkable," they all declared.

Jenny didn't think it was remarkable. She was angry, as Jo had expected she would be.

"That's not your Talent," Jenny had hissed at her fiancé. Jo listened through the front window, her toes anchored against the porch to stop the creak of the swing from betraying her.

"But no one was using it," Juan had argued. "Don't you think Talents are meant to be used? Joley said . . ." Jo wasn't sure if

Juan trailed off then, or if his words simply grew too quiet to hear.

The argument continued so long into the night that when Jo's parents found her, she was curled on the porch swing, asleep.

Jenny and Juan did not get married. Jenny returned his engagement ring, but left him the watch. By then, word of Juan's Talent had spread far beyond postmen and barbers, and soon he left on a six-month world tour. He found a new love, Jo read in the magazines, and started a new family, and with each new tour, his fame grew greater. El Picaflor, they called him. The Hummingbird. Journalists were particularly fascinated by his beautiful pocket watch—his good luck charm, they wrote, never suspecting the truth behind it—and how he wound it carefully before each performance, and kept it in a special glass case when he slept or bathed, so no dust or moisture would muss its gears.

Jenny, in turn, forged a much quieter life for herself. Jo picked up snippets of information here and there, from news articles or bits of gossip around town. Jenny had named her orphanage Miss Mallory's Home for Lost Girls. She'd found a daughter, Cady, and a home in a peanut butter factory, of all places. But no matter how much time passed, Jenny never forgot the original thought that had wiggled a crack into her relationship, and the person who had planted it.

Jo had tried to stop the future from coming, but it came.

Which was why, when she'd found those first jars at the edge of the lake five summers ago, glowing yellow-purple, hope had finally risen in her chest. If Jenny couldn't forget on her own, maybe Jo could help her along a little.

There was a knock on the office door.

"And you are?" Jo asked, tugging it open. The girl before her was short and slim, with light brown skin and shoulder-length brown hair. Hers was a familiar face, although one at the very edges of Jo's memory.

The girl gulped. "I'm Lily," she said. "Liliana."

The Pinnacle, Jo remembered now. She'd seen her photo on the camp application. "And what is it that you need, Liliana?"

Lily wound a swampy length of yarn around her thumb. "I was hoping," she said slowly, "that you could give me a Talent bracelet."

In one swift movement, Jo yanked Lily into the office, slamming the door behind them.

"I don't know what she told you." Jo could tell that the finger she was jabbing in the girl's face was making her nervous. Good. "But it's lies, all of it."

"What wh-who told me?" Lily stammered.

Jo wasn't buying the act. "There are no Talent bracelets here," she said. And that, at least for the moment, was the truth. "So you can scurry on back to your cabin and stop bothering me."

"B-But," Lily said, "I was standing right here." She pointed to the spot on the floor where, mere moments ago, Jo had finished sweeping. "And I dropped the jar. And the frog swallowed the bracelet, and then he was . . . *Talented*. The glass shattered all over my green high—"

Even as she spoke the words, Lily seemed confused by them. As though she'd begun watching a movie halfway through and couldn't quite piece together the plot. She frowned at her faded brown sneakers.

"*You* broke the jar?" Jo asked, hope rising in her chest.

"Yes," Lily said. "I was standing right there." But she seemed less certain with every word. "Wasn't I?"

Jo placed an arm on the girl's shoulder. "Honey," she said, with all the sweetness she could muster, "I think you're having some sort of episode. Why don't you lie down for a bit?"

"An episode?" Lily asked.

"If it persists, have Nurse Bonnie take your temperature." And she pressed Lily out of the office.

Well, how about that? Jo thought, patting Grandma Esther's harmonica in her sweater pocket. After all this time, after all her searching, Fate had sent her a Recollector.

Jo quickly got to work.

Dear Jenny, she wrote. *Of all the letters I've written you, this is the most important.*

A Recollector could take memories from one person—the way Chuck had had her memory taken, right before Jo's eyes—and, if he or she wanted to, give those memories to somebody else—the way Lily had been given a memory that most certainly wasn't hers.

No matter what may have happened between us, I need to you to come now. It's crucial that I see you.

It wasn't so much the giving of memories that Jo was interested in.

Next Sunday, she wrote, in her neat blocky letters. *After my campers' Talent show.* That ought to give her plenty of time.

> *I'm begging you, Jenny. Please come. I want*
> *nothing more than to be a family again.*
>
> *Your sister,*
>
> Jo

Jo folded the letter into thirds and slid it into an envelope for Del's next mail run.

Jenny would come. She had to. And when she did, she'd forget why she'd never come before. All Jo had to do was ensure that the Recollector, whoever the person was, took a good, long dip in the lake.

Passing beneath the moose head keeping guard above the lodge's double doors, Jo stepped into the sunlight and pulled Grandma Esther's harmonica to her lips.

Turquoise, plum, salmon, teal. Marigold, coral, slate, snow. With every camper Jo played for, she saw colors. An abundance of Singular Talents.

"Renny, that's her again," Jo heard a camper whine. "She'll make us go in the lake."

"You don't have to go swimming, Miles," came the reply.

"No water!"

Miles shouted the words just as Jo turned to face him, her harmonica at her lips.

Pearl, alabaster, porcelain, frost. She drew in a breath of surprise, making the colors even more vivid. She never would have guessed if she hadn't seen it for herself.

Miles Patrick Francis Fennelbridge, the disappointment of his family, was a Recollector.

"No water!" Miles flicked his fingers. *Flick-flick-flick-flick-flick!*

Jo stopped playing. Pulled her harmonica down from her mouth. Blinked at the bright afternoon sky.

There was an itch, just below her ear.

She glanced at the harmonica in her hands, certain she'd been playing it only moments earlier, but befuddled as to why.

"Jo?"

When she looked up, Jo saw Del, her head counselor.

"Teagan asked me to give this to you," Del said, holding out a thick white envelope. Jo took it and peeked inside. It was the money Caleb had given her earlier. She scratched below her ear. "Got anything for the mail run?"

There was a hint of something lingering in her mind. A

memory, perhaps, although Jo could only catch the flavor of a few remaining tendrils.

It tasted of buttered popcorn.

Jo slipped her harmonica back into her sweater pocket and found a letter there, addressed to her sister. *Expedited mail*, she'd written on the front, in her neat blocky letters.

"Here." She handed it to Del.

There was something Jo had been looking for, she thought, as she headed back to her office. No—something she'd *found*. But for the life of her, she couldn't remember what it was.

Sometimes memories hit like a wallop, all of sudden, and hard. Other times, for no reason that anyone can explain, memories take much longer to sink in. They seem to meander a bit before choosing which mind to settle into.

As Jo made her way back to the lodge, her buttered-popcorn memory was doing an awful lot of meandering. It tickled the tops of the pine trees, dove back down to the dirt, and darted here and there between the feet of Camp Atropos's many campers. It meandered throughout the evening, after the sun had set, then spent several days perched on a branch below a nest of friendly birds. Eventually, it would find where it wanted to be. But it was in no rush.

Some memories are slower than others.

—

The Following Week . . .

Lily

LILY LAY ON HER BACK, HER ARMS TUCKED INSIDE HER sleeping bag, warm in the chill of the morning, spinning a post-card in circles above her. The sun had only barely poked itself into the sky, and her bunkmates were all still snoring.

Hallo from Johannesburg! the postcard read, in her father's tight scrawl. *Looking forward to seeing you Sunday!*

For the past eleven days, Lily had been trying to come up with some sort of phenomenal act for her and Max to perform at the Talent show. She'd tried levitating Max's hair into amazing new hairdos, but none of the hairdos were quite amazing enough. She'd attempted a game of flying pinochle, but that hadn't ended well for anybody. And then there was the unfortunate juice-juggling incident that got Lily banned from the infirmary for an entire afternoon.

"I'll just help Hannah with her punch," Max had told Lily yesterday. "Really, I don't mind. You should help, too. Everyone will get to drink it and have good memories. It'll be a nice thing for everybody."

"I do plenty of nice things for everybody," Lily had grumbled in reply. Although, as soon as she'd said it, she couldn't think of a single example. "Punch is dumb," she finished lamely.

Lily curled the sleep out of her toes, her thoughts focused as the postcard circled above her.

Looking forward to seeing you Sunday!

Just two short days.

If only Jo really *were* keeping Talent bracelets in her office. The dream Lily had had last week—the "episode," Jo had called it—felt so real that Lily could taste it.

Peaches. It tasted like peaches.

But Lily knew that what she remembered couldn't be real, because in the dream, the jar had shattered across the toes of her Kelly-green high-tops, and Lily had never in her life owned a pair of—

Lily let the postcard flutter to her chest. *Chuck*, she realized. Chuck hadn't worn those green shoes since the first morning of camp, but Lily had seen her in them. She was certain of it.

Focusing her thoughts at the bridge of her nose, Lily pulled back her sleeping bag. Carefully, quietly, she slid off the top bunk to the floor, being sure not to wake Chuck on the bed below. In the next bunk over, Miles slept flat on his stomach on his bottom bed, while above him Renny was curled into a tight ball. On the far side of the room, Ellie lay all alone, her left hand grazing the floor.

Crouching on her hands and knees, Lily peered beneath the bed, where Chuck had a habit of stuffing her things. Sure enough, behind a damp beach towel, Lily spotted a single Kelly-green high-top. She focused her thoughts at the bridge of her nose and tugged the shoe out.

Lily hadn't dreamed it at all. Someone had given her Chuck Holloway's memory.

The sun painted the dirt path orange as Lily hurried toward the lodge. The woods were filled with the music of an early summer morning—birds chirping, leaves rustling, squirrels *yut-yut-yut*ting. Otherwise, the camp was still. Lily scuttled to Jo's office window. She couldn't see past the curtain inside, and the window itself was—she tried it—locked.

But locked windows were no match for a Pinnacle.

Focusing her thoughts at the bridge of her nose, Lily concentrated on the window's latch, through the glass pane. Slowly, it began to twist. With the window unlocked, Lily shifted her focus and pulled the window up. *Cre-eeeak!* The noise was thunderous in the quiet of the camp. Lily tensed her shoulders, waiting, but the only sounds she heard were the birds, the leaves, the squirrels.

Lily pulled the window open.

Pushing the curtain to one side, Lily peered inside the office. She didn't need to look far. The shelves that lined the wall were bursting with glass jars, each of them sample-size, no larger than a Ping-Pong ball. Hundreds and hundreds of jars. And each, Lily could see as she leaned farther inside, had a bracelet nestled at the bottom, red or purple or yellow. Each jar was labeled, too, with a strip of masking tape, although even when she squinted, the words didn't make much sense to Lily.

FROGS—that's what was written on one of the labels.

HAIR, read another.

Focusing her thoughts at the bridge of her nose, Lily lifted a jar from the bottom shelf, where Jo would be least likely to miss it, and tugged it toward her through the air. The bracelet in the jar was orange, Max's favorite color, and the label read HEAT.

As Lily eased the window shut, she failed to notice that one jar with a bright green bracelet inside teetered off its perch. She didn't observe it rolling across the office floor.

And she certainly didn't see the jar wedge itself deep beneath Jo's filing cabinet.

• • •

"I brought you something," Lily told Max when she got to the infirmary. Nurse Bonnie had gone to grab breakfast, so they were alone for the moment.

Lily pulled the jar from her pocket and unscrewed the lid. Then she pinched the orange bracelet between two fingers— she didn't want the Talent to soak into her own skin and go to waste.

"A bracelet?" Max said, wrinkling his nose when he saw her gift.

"Orange is your favorite color," Lily reminded him, stretching his arm taut. She wondered what the label HEAT meant. Controlling the temperature might make for a nice act, or even knowing how hot it was outside without a thermometer. Lily tied the bracelet around Max's wrist.

"Where'd you get it, anyway?" Max asked, examining the orange thread against his light brown skin.

Lily wound her own length of swampy yarn around her thumb, waiting for Max's new Talent to soak through to his bones. It hadn't taken long at all, she remembered, with the frog.

"I made it," she lied. "Arts and craf—"

"Look what I have for you!" came the world's most annoying voice. Hannah's long blond hair swished behind her as she stepped through the gap in the curtains. She was holding some sort of bright green concoction, in a tall clear glass.

Max straightened himself in the bed. "What is it?" he said. And Lily hated that his eyes lit up for the green muck Hannah brought him, when they hadn't for her bracelet.

"Wait till you see," Hannah told him, holding out the glass.

It happened quickly.

One second, Max was holding the glass, bringing it in for a sip.

The next second, he said, "Oh." Very quietly, but Lily heard it. And his eyes were wide. Worried.

The next second after that, Lily saw the first bubble, on the surface of the green juice. It burst with an audible *pop!*

In the second that followed, more bubbles appeared. More and more and more. Until, only five seconds after it had all begun, the juice was boiling over, splashing out of the glass, sticky and scalding, and Max shrieked, and Hannah screamed, too, and Lily leapt to her feet, and the glass smashed to the ground, spraying boiling green muck everywhere.

"What *happened*?" Hannah cried, grabbing for Max's hands. They were unnaturally red. Swollen. Max howled, tears welling in his eyes.

"I have no ide—"

Lily's fingers clasped around the small glass jar.

HEAT—that's what was written on the top.

"I'll find Nurse Bonnie," Lily said. And she raced out of the room, out of the infirmary, running, running, kicking up dirt along the path to the lodge. She took the steps to the mess deck two at a time, and pressed through the campers crowded in the breakfast line. She spotted Chuck and Ellie near the front.

"No cutting!" called a kid behind her, but Lily ignored him.

"Have you seen Nurse Bonnie?" Lily asked the twins.

"Are you sick?" Ellie asked.

"Haven't seen her," Chuck replied. "Why is this line *taking* so long?"

Still searching the crowd, Lily followed Chuck's gaze to the far end of the breakfast line. A group was clustered at the beverage station watching one of the older campers, Hal—who was thirteen or fourteen, and large, with an unfortunate bowl haircut—take a cup of ice water. "Let's see this mind-blowing Talent show act," the counselor Teagan told him. And, with the drama of a magician performing a card trick, Hal took the cup, raising his eyebrows at his audience.

Lily could see it even from where she stood—the bubbles at the top of the cup. The beverage was boiling between Hal's hands.

With a flourish, Hal poured in a sprinkling of hot cocoa powder, and gave the cup's contents a quick stir with a plastic spoon. "There you are," he told Teagan, handing over the cup. "Faster than a microwave."

Teagan's hair shifted from electric blue bob to stark white, growing six inches. "Very nice," she told Hal.

"His act's going to be *so* much better than identifying frogs," Chuck said, turning back to Lily with a sigh.

Around and around Lily wound the length of yarn at her thumb. Suddenly lots of new thoughts were clamoring for space in her brain.

She looked at Chuck and Ellie. The Frog Twins, everyone called them.

FROGS.

That had been written on one of the jars in Jo's office.

Lily's gaze shifted to Teagan, now sporting a blond pixie cut.

HAIR.

That was one, too.

And finally Lily's eyes settled on Hal, who was bowing for his adoring audience.

HEAT.

Lily wound the length of swampy yarn around and around her thumb, working it faster and faster.

"Lily?" Ellie said. "Are you okay?"

Something strange was going on at Camp Atropos. Something very, very strange.

Lily just had to figure out *what*.

Chuck's Frozen Mint Hot Chocolate

— a drink reminiscent of a cool swim on a hot day —

FOR THE FROZEN HOT CHOCOLATE:
- 1 ½ cups whole milk, divided
- 6 sprigs fresh mint (plus more for garnish if desired)
- ⅔ cup semisweet chocolate chips
- 1 tbsp unsweetened cocoa powder
- 3 tbsp sugar
- 5 cups ice
- whipped cream (optional)

1. In a small saucepan, combine ½ cup of the milk and 6 sprigs of mint. Heat on the lowest setting for 4 minutes, stirring constantly and smashing the mint into the milk. Do not let the mixture boil.

2. Using tongs or a fork, remove the mint sprigs from the milk and discard them.

3. Add the chocolate chips, cocoa powder, and sugar to the milk. Stirring constantly, continue heating on the lowest setting until the chocolate melts and the mixture is smooth, 3 to 5 minutes.

4. Remove the chocolate mixture from the heat. Stir in the remaining 1 cup milk, mixing well.

5. Put the ice in the blender and carefully pour in the chocolate mixture. Blend on high until smooth. Pour into two tall glasses and top with whipped cream and fresh mint sprigs, if desired. Serve with drinking straws or spoons.

[Serves 2]

Chuck

HER CHEEKS PUFFED WIDE AND HER EYES SQUEEZED tight, Chuck dunked her head beneath the surface of Lake Atropos, letting the chill prickle her skin through her swimsuit. Every day, it seemed, the lake grew colder and colder, as though some water-warming spell it had been enchanted with was quickly wearing off. But Chuck didn't mind so much. Since the morning they'd arrived at camp, the only seconds she'd had to herself were the ones she spent underwater.

"Hey, Chuck!" Ellie cried, as soon as Chuck popped her head above the surface. "Want to leave free swim early to practice for the Talent show?" Chuck drew fresh air into her straining lungs. "Dress rehearsal's tomorrow, and we've got a *lot* of work to do."

"I want to swim."

"But we really need to work on the act," Ellie argued, wind-milling her arms and legs to stay upright in the water. "I still need to show you how to—"

"I'm going to play Squid," Chuck cut in. And she dove beneath the surface again, splashing as she swam for the wooden plat-form floating farther out in the water, where a few dozen campers and counselors were gathered.

Ellie followed her, of course. But Chuck did her best not to be bothered.

The rules of Squid were simple. One person acted as a "squid" and sat at the edge of the platform with her toes in the water, guarding "Neptune's gold"—which was really, in this case, a pair of swim goggles perched on the platform behind her. The other players tried to grab the gold, but if the squid tagged one of them first, then that player became part of the squid's "tenta-cles," holding on to the squid's hands or feet. As more players were tagged, the tentacles grew longer, stretching far out into the water in all directions, and it became more difficult to get the gold. The player to grab the goggles became the new squid.

The first round went quickly. A girl named Molly was the squid, and she put up a noble effort to guard the gold, but little Gracie was using her Talent for lie-detecting to know when Molly was fibbing about how far she could reach, and one of the boys, Jason, could hold his breath for up to seventeen minutes, so no one ever knew where or when he was going to pop up from under the water.

"This is fun, Chuck," Ellie said, grabbing tight to her hand as they rested for a moment at the edge of the platform. Chuck's arm grew chilly as she soaked in their shared Talent. There were ninety-seven frogs swimming along the southernmost bank of Lake Atropos at that moment. Fifty-five male, the rest female. Seven different species. "Playing Squid was a good idea."

Chuck released her hand from Ellie's grip, then immediately squeezed the Talent back.

During the second round of the game, with Jason as the squid, Chuck was tagged right away. She took her place as Jason's tentacle—her right hand in his left—wishing she had a Talent of her own. Something that she didn't have to share with Ellie. Something utterly unique, like that silver knot she kept in her shorts pocket. Quirky and complicated and beautiful. Was that too much to ask?

An icy chill trickled up Chuck's arm, precisely the same feeling she got when the frog Talent passed to her from Ellie. Only it wasn't Ellie's hand Chuck was holding.

It was Jason's.

Chuck gasped in surprise, and when she did, her lungs—she could feel them—they *expanded*. Right inside her chest.

She glanced at Jason, still sitting on the platform, still trying to tag the other campers. He looked exactly the same as he had a moment earlier. But Chuck couldn't shake the feeling that perhaps he wasn't, really. That perhaps *she* wasn't.

Chuck sank below the water, *down down down*.

A long minute passed. Maybe two. Chuck opened her eyes, watching the fish swim past her in the murky water.

"Are you *okay?*" Ellie asked her, when she managed to tug Chuck above the surface. "I thought you were *drowning.* You were down there for *so long.*"

"I was?" Her lungs didn't ache. Not in the slightest.

Chuck squeezed Jason's Talent back into his arm, warm like hot chocolate.

"Hey, Ellie?" she asked her sister, kicking her legs underneath her. "Have you ever been able to share a Talent with anyone else? Besides me, I mean?"

Ellie squinted at her, water dripping off her hundreds of braids onto the straps of her swimsuit. "Are you sure you weren't down there too long?"

"Never mind," Chuck said.

In the third round of the game, Teagan was the squid, sitting on the platform in front of the goggles, her hair shifting from black to red to purple as she taunted the campers. Chuck let herself be tagged on purpose. She went to join little strawberry-haired Gracie, who was hanging on to Teagan's left hand. And, the instant Chuck thought about soaking up a new Talent, it happened.

The icy spark climbed Chuck's arm, the Talent for lie-detecting sprinting into her chest. When Jason swore he wouldn't sneak underwater, Chuck knew for certain he was lying. Chuck was so overwhelmed with her new ability, it took her a moment to notice that Teagan's hair—which mere moments ago had been a black-and-white checkerboard, reaching out at all angles to tag swimming campers—was now a perfectly plain brown. Slightly frizzy. Pulled back behind her ears.

But even stranger than that was the sight of *Gracie's* hair. With one hand gripping Teagan's and the other clutched in Chuck's, Gracie's usual strawberry hair was slowly turning . . . *violet*.

In a blink, Gracie's hair returned to normal. But Chuck was certain she had seen it. Somehow, Gracie had absorbed Teagan's Talent, just as Chuck had absorbed hers. Somehow—

A second icy spark crept up Chuck's arm.

While everyone else was focused on the platform, where Molly had just snatched the gold, Chuck shifted her gaze to her shoulder, her breathing heavy. There was a peculiar tickling at her neck.

Chuck's sweepy black cornrows were slowly, *slowly*, unwinding. She could see them from the corner of her eye, even though normally they didn't reach past her chin. Her cornrows were *growing*, and they were turning *green*. Pistachio green. As the campers watched Molly's victory dance and Chuck did her best not to faint right into the water, her hair wove itself into one long, thick green braid.

Shocked, Chuck let go of Gracie's hand. And then, on a hunch, she grabbed it again.

It wasn't ice this time that traveled through her, but warmth, like a bath after a day of sledding. The Talent gushed out of Chuck's chest, back down the length of her arm, and back into Gracie's hand. Beside her, Gracie—still focused on the platform and the dancing—rolled her shoulders as though something peculiar had passed through them. Her hair began to change again, working its way into a tangerine Mohawk, and still she kept laughing, none the wiser. Chuck squeezed harder, and Gracie's hair went back to normal, and then Teagan, still tentacle-gripped with Gracie, transformed from a normally coiffed counselor to checkerboard crazy once more. At the same time, Chuck could feel the warmth of the lie-detecting Talent leaving her chest, working its way back to its rightful owner.

Chuck dropped Gracie's hand and dunked herself fully under the water again, letting the coolness envelop her, trying to gather her thoughts.

All this time, Chuck thought. All this time, Chuck had assumed she and Ellie shared a Talent for identifying frogs. But—she kicked down into the chilly depths a little harder— what if Chuck had never had the frog Talent at all? What if it had been Ellie's all along, and Chuck had merely borrowed it, just as she'd borrowed Gracie's a moment ago? Just as she'd borrowed Teagan's, and Jason's?

Maybe, Chuck thought as she kicked for shore, ignoring Ellie's hollering behind her, she wasn't a Frog Twin. Maybe she never had been.

Maybe, just maybe, she was something a little more . . .

Unique.

Renny

"**You know, I picked you for my team, Fennelbridge,**" Hal grumbled, tossing a plastic water bottle between his two hands, "because I thought you'd be able to tell me where the Blue Team hid their flag."

"That would be cheating," Renny replied, tugging at the top of his right sock.

Miles had insisted on sitting out of Capture the Flag, because one side of the field backed up onto the lake. ("*No water!*" he'd shouted, and Renny had needed to grab hold of his fingers to stop the flicking.) So now, after gobbling down three Caramel Crème bars and handing the empty wrappers to Renny, Miles was passing his afternoon examining bugs at the edge of the field farthest from the water.

"That's cheating, too, by the way," Renny told Hal, pointing at the team captain's water bottle. Whenever members of the Blue Team neared the rock that hid the Red Team's flag, Hal would heat up the water and use it to chase them off.

Hal rolled his eyes at Renny. "It's called Camp Atropos for Singular Talents. Not Camp Atropos for Losers Who Don't Use Their Talents. Anyway, you don't hear me complaining about Del." Hal pointed to the Blue Team's half of the field, where the head counselor had used his Numbing Talent to turn the remnants of last night's rain into a slippery slush. Most of the Red Team's best players had skidded onto their rear ends in it, which was why they were now languishing in their enemies' jail. "And I'm pretty positive Nolan hid their flag so high up that tree that no one but him can get it down. Just admit that you can't actually read minds."

Renny bent down to tug at the top of his sock again. "I know what's in your back pocket," he said.

Hal snorted. "That's stupid."

Renny merely shrugged, like he dealt with morons who didn't believe in his incredible Scanner ability every day. "I'll bet you ten dollars."

"Fine," Hal said, although he was clearly still skeptical. "Ten dollars. What have I got in my pocket?"

"Three Caramel Crème bars," Renny replied.

At that, Hal laughed. "I think you meant to get on the bus to Fair Camp," he said, reaching a hand to his back pocket.

"Because there definitely are *not* any Caramel Crème—" He stopped talking when he pulled out the wrappers, the chocolate smeared across his fingertips. "Why, you little—"

From his own pocket, Renny removed Hal's wallet, which he'd swiped several minutes earlier. "I already took out the ten bucks," he told Hal. "That'll buy Miles a lot of candy." If the Caramel Crème company really was going to stop production on the candy bars soon, like Teagan had said, then Renny figured he better buy up as many of the things as possible. He tossed Hal the wallet. "Thanks."

Renny expected Hal to try to slug him then, or to throw his hot water bottle at him, at least. So he was surprised when the wallop hit the *back* of his head.

Hal seemed surprised, too. "What the—?" he began, as Renny whirled around.

The pebble was still floating in the air, small and round and black, fluttering like a bird. Tied around it with a thin length of swampy yarn was a scrap of notebook paper. As Renny and Hal watched, silent, the green yarn untied itself and then the paper unwrapped itself, too.

I need your help.

Once Renny had read it, the note crumpled itself into a ball and dropped to the ground, but the pebble kept floating. Renny tugged it out of the air, following the length of swampy yarn as it floated past Miles in the grass (*"Can I get another Caramel Crème bar?"*), deep into the shadows of the trees.

"Hey! You can't just leave in the middle of the game!" Hal shouted from the field.

When Renny reached Lily in the trees, he waved the pebble at her. "Most people tap me on the shoulder when they want my attention."

Lily held out her thumb, and the small length of swampy yarn wrapped itself around it, tying itself into a knot. "I need you to read Jo's mind," she told him. "She's dangerous."

"The camp director?" Renny raised his eyebrows. So far all Jo had done was insist that he go swimming a lot, and that hardly seemed like something to worry about. He rubbed the back of his head, still sore from its run-in with the rock. "I think *you're* more dangerous than she is."

"Did you know there's a Recollector at this camp?" Lily asked him.

Despite the heat of the afternoon, Renny's body went cold. He glanced back at Miles, who was lying on his belly in the grass now, staring at bugs.

"One of the counselors or someone, I don't know who," Lily went on. "Somebody gave me a memory, a really important one, so that I could do something about it. Don't you think that doing something to stop a dangerous Mimic is a much better way to help the whole camp than making punch?"

Renny rubbed the warmth back into his arms. Lily didn't know about Miles. "I have to get back to the game," Renny told her.

"Jo's a *Mimic*," Lily insisted. "She must be. She's been copying our Talents. Us campers, I mean. This whole time. She has hundreds of Talent bracelets in her office. In jars, Renny. Just sitting in jars."

"Jars?" Renny asked.

"I need you to read her mind to figure out how she's doing it. You know it's illegal, right? To Mimic people's Talents without telling them? And people could get hurt, Renny. People have already gotten . . ." Lily wound the length of yarn around her thumb.

"You're positive she has copies of Talents?" Renny asked. "Good ones?"

Lily nodded. "Jars and jars of them," she said. "Will you help?"

Buttered popcorn.

The memory hit Renny suddenly, as though it had plopped directly into his mind from the tree above him. Renny scratched below his ear, where the buttered-popcorn memory seemed to have settled.

Renny had been playing his harmonica, he remembered, scratching. His grandma Esther's harmonica.

Which was peculiar, because he didn't remember having a grandma Esther.

Scratch scratch scratch. Renny had been looking for something. No. *Scratch scratch.* He'd *found* something.

Renny whipped around, his gaze landing on Miles, belly down in the grass.

Pearl, alabaster, porcelain, frost. Renny remembered seeing the colors dancing above Miles's head. He'd seen them with the harmonica. *Scratch scratch.*

Jo had been looking for Miles.

"Renny?" Lily said again. Around and around she wound the yarn at her thumb. "Are you going to help me or not?"

Jars and jars of Talents, he thought. He stopped scratching the buttered-popcorn memory.

"No," he said at last. "I'm going to help somebody else."

Lily

"THE LINE MUST BE BREAKING UP," LILY'S MOTHER SAID.

Lily pressed the receiver hard into her cheek, and tried to make herself as small as possible against the lodge wall. The only public phone in all of Camp Atropos was located just outside the door to Jo's office, and you had to get Del's permission to use it. Luckily, Del had left her alone when she said she needed to discuss a personal matter with her parents.

"I can't quite hear what you're saying, Lily Belle," her mom went on.

"I heard her fine," Lily's stepfather, Steve, replied. Lily could picture them perfectly, sitting at the kitchen table with her mom's mobile between them, on speakerphone. Lily's mother, a Talented multitasker, would be drafting a shopping list and mending a hole in Steve's sweater while mopping a coffee spill with her foot, and Steve would be twisting apart a sandwich cookie. He could do it perfectly every time, so that all the cream ended up on one side, no messy breaks. "Lily told us that their camp director is a Mimic, and she's duplicating all their Talents. Stuffing them into jars."

"Oh, I heard *that*," Lily's mom said. "I just thought it was so ridiculous there must be something wrong with the phone. You still have *your* Talent, don't you, Lily Belle?"

"Mimics don't *take* Talents, Mom," Lily said. She focused her thoughts at the bridge of her nose and turned her gaze to the moose head keeping guard above the lodge's double doors. Just to check, she budged one of his eyes closed, then open. "They *copy* them."

"Lily Belle, it's perfectly natural to get homesick. There's no need to make up stories. If you want us to come pick you up, we're happy to do it. Although we'll see you on Sunday, you know, at the Talent show."

"Wouldn't miss it!" Steve chimed in, a little too cheerily. "I hear Hannah and Max are making punch."

"Max is *not* making punch," Lily shot back. But there were heavier things on her mind. "Max got hurt," she said. Around and around went the length of yarn. That night, Lily knew, after the campfire, the lodge would be packed full of kids for the all-camp slumber party, but at the moment, it was so empty that her words bounced off the walls.

(*Max got hurt. Max got hurt. Max got hurt.*)

"Nurse Bonnie told us about the accident with the juice," Steve said calmly. "But Max is fine now. We talked to him a half hour ago. Nurse Bonnie has a Talent for salves. She said he's fine to attend the slumber party tonight and everything."

"How's Hannah doing?" Lily's mother cut in. "Has she been occupying herself during free swim?"

Who cared what Hannah was doing during free swim? "I'm going to go," Lily replied.

"All right. Bye, Lily Belle. See you on Sun—"

Lily called her father next.

"Liria!" her father said, as soon as he picked up the phone. Lily loved the way he said his nickname for her, with the lilt on the first syllable. "Bonjour from Marseilles! To what do I owe this pleasure?"

Lily didn't waste any time. Told her father the whole story—minus a few details—about the Talent bracelet and the stealing.

"Oh, Liria," he said when she'd finished. "If you don't like camp, why don't you call your mother and have her pick you up?"

"But . . ." She should've known her father wouldn't think her problems were big enough to rearrange his schedule for. Lily sighed. "Couldn't you come a little early? I mean, you were planning on coming Sunday anyway, right? For the Talent show?"

In the pause that followed, Lily knew what the answer was, without even needing the words. She'd heard enough pauses in her life.

"I'm so sorry, Liria," her father said at last. And he did, truly, sound sorry, but that didn't fix things, did it? "You know that traveling helps ease my heartache."

Lily placed the receiver back in its cradle on the wall. And then, so softly that even the empty lodge wouldn't repeat it, Lily whispered, "What about mine?"

If no one was going to help her, Lily decided, then she was going to have to help everybody.

Taking two steps toward Jo's office and the hundreds of jars locked inside, Lily focused her thoughts at the bridge of her nose. Slowly, through the door, she lifted every last jar—one inch, then two—off the shelf.

"You work things out okay?" came a voice from behind her.

Lily swiveled around, her heart pummeling against her ribs. Behind the office door, the jars settled back onto their shelves with a soft series of *clank!*s.

Del turned his head to the noise, then back to Lily.

"Oh," Lily said, catching her breath. "Oh, yeah. Everything's fine now, thanks."

She eyed the office door again, then glanced at Del.

"You want to join your cabinmates at archery?" he asked her.

Around and around Lily wound the yarn at her thumb. "Um," she said. *Around and around.* "Sure." And she crossed the lodge floor, passing beneath the moose head and down the steps to the dirt path.

Tonight, she thought, scurrying through shade-then-light-then-shade-again. Tonight, when everyone was at the campfire, she'd have her chance.

Liliana Vera was going to help *everybody.*

Renny

"BUT WE'RE SUPPOSED TO BE REHEARSING FOR THE Talent show," Miles said as they bustled through the trees toward the lodge. "It's the last day before dress rehearsal." Cabin Twelve had taken over the flag circle, Cabin Twenty-Six was at the archery ring, and the rest of the Cabin Eight campers were at the arts-and-crafts cabin. But Del had told Renny that Jo was in her office, so that's where he and Miles were headed. Besides, Renny didn't need any more practice at faking a Talent.

"We're *supposed* to be *rehearsing*," Miles said again. Renny could see the tip of Miles's pinkie beginning to twitch.

"You're not even technically in the Talent show," Renny reasoned, grabbing for his brother's hand. "You just help out from the audience." How great would it be to have a real act for the Talent show? To see his parents' faces light up when he performed? To read something they'd said about him in one of their interviews and not feel his gut twist inside him, knowing it was a lie?

Renny knocked and knocked on Jo's office door, but no one answered. Miles watched the kids from Cabin Thirty-Three, who were rehearsing on the stage at the far end of the lodge. A girl named Molly was telling time perfectly, down to the second, without glancing at a clock.

"Two-oh-seven!" she cried, popping her eyes open. "And eighteen seconds. Nineteen."

"*Renny*," Miles whined again, "I really think we're supposed to be *rehearsing*."

Renny pounded harder on the door—so hard that he didn't hear the footsteps behind him.

"Can I help you?"

Renny squared his shoulders as he turned, pretending that Jo didn't scare him in the slightest. "I know you're looking for the Recollector Talent," he told her. Sometimes the best approach was an honest one. "And I know where you can find it."

Jo scratched a spot below one ear. She looked as though she were trying to fit a piece into a puzzle that she hadn't realized she was missing. When at last the puzzle piece seemed to snap into place, Jo pulled her harmonica from her sweater pocket and lifted it to her lips.

"I can play the harmonica," Miles informed them. "I learned last year in music class."

"I know, Miles. *Shh*," Renny whispered.

Jo played a melancholy tune, her eyes set on Miles. Renny recognized the song from the radio.

Los golpes en la vida
preparan nuestros corazones
como el fuego forja al acero.

"*Miles Fennelbridge,*" Jo breathed.

"Miles Patrick Francis Fennelbridge," Miles began. Renny could tell just from the tone of his voice that his brother was reciting Talent history again. "Thirteen years old as of his last birthday. Talent: Recollector." He looked up at Jo, his eyes suddenly wide with worry. "Renny and I have a brother bond. So you can't tell anyone."

The way Jo smiled at Miles, you'd think he was a particularly tasty-looking tuna she'd spied in a fish shop. "Not a soul," she assured him.

Then she fixed her gaze on Renny.

"I need that Talent," she said, dropping the harmonica into her sweater pocket.

Miles slipped back into his recitation. "Dorothy Ida Whitaker. Born 1880, died 1899. Talent: Tapissier."

"Miles can take any memory for you," Renny told Jo. "Or give you one, if that's what you want. He's good at it, if I help him. Give me a Talent bracelet, and he'll do it. I know you have some."

(*"Able to weave dreams into cloth,"* Miles went on. *"Fun fact: For a fee, visitors to the Talent Library in Munich, Germany, can take a nap beneath one of Dorothy Whitaker's blankets."*)

"Your brother can't be trusted with something so sensitive," Jo told Renny. "If you want to negotiate with me, Renwick Fennelbridge, you'll need to get me my own copy of that Talent."

Renny tugged at the top of his right sock. "A copy?"

In response, Jo pulled out a key and unlocked her office. She swung the door open wide, so Renny could see. "I'll give you any Talent you want," she told him.

Hundreds and hundreds of jars lined the shelf on the wall. Each held a bracelet, and each jar's lid was labeled with neat blocky letters.

"Those are all . . . ?" Renny began.

"Talents," she told him. "Not a bad one in the bunch."

Renny glanced at Miles, who was still busy reciting. (*"Thomas Alphonse Martin. Born 1776, died 1875. Talent: Fledgling."*) Then he turned back to Jo.

"How do I get you a copy?" he asked.

Chuck

CHUCK CROUCHED, SHOULDERS TENSED, BEHIND THE rickety equipment shed, eyes darting to her feet. Her water shoes were still drenched from the lake, so she'd squirmed under her bunk to retrieve her Kelly-green high-tops. Somehow, they didn't bother her anymore. Because even if she looked a little froggy, Chuck knew she was an utterly unique individual.

An utterly unique individual who was currently hiding from her identical twin sister.

(*Please just be in the Talent show with me anyway, Chuck.* That's what Ellie would say if Chuck tried to tell her what she'd discovered at the lake. *Please, Chuck? Please?* And Ellie would frown when she said it, too. *Here, Chuck, take my hand, and we'll talk to some frogs. Chuck? Chuck?*)

When the voices on the path drifted farther away, Chuck poked her head out from behind the shed. It was only Renny and Miles with Jo, heading toward the lake.

Chuck clenched and unclenched her hand. She was dying to experiment, to discover precisely what she could do with her Talent. So far Chuck knew what she wasn't: a Frog Twin. Now she needed to discover what she *was*.

(*Please, Chuck? Please?*)

Once she knew for sure, Chuck told herself—once she discovered exactly what she was—she wasn't going to hide anymore. She was going to tell everyone. She'd shimmy right up the flagpole, even, and announce it to the world. Chuck didn't care how hard Ellie would frown when she announced it, either. She didn't.

She didn't.

The campfire. Chuck would have a chance to figure things out at the campfire.

In the meantime, she hid behind the equipment shed, clenching and unclenching her hand.

Renny

IN A MILLION YEARS, RENNY NEVER WOULD HAVE GUESSED that he'd find himself paddling a canoe in the middle of a lake with his older brother. But if he ever *had* guessed it, he would have predicted that it would be exactly this horrible.

"*No water.*" Miles's voice was a trembly, terrifying whisper. His knuckles were white as he clutched the sides of the canoe, his chest heaving underneath his orange life vest. "*No water.*"

Flick-flick-flick-flick-flick! went his fingers against the wood.

"It's okay," Renny told him as he paddled. He tried his best to sound comforting. "It's only water, Miles. And I'm right here."

Miles pulled his gaze away from the murky water. "You're right here," he repeated, his eyes wide and wet.

"Why don't you tell me some Talent history?" Renny said. "How about old Howard Greenspan?"

"Howard Greenspan," Miles started. "Thirty"—he let out a tiny *whelp!* as the canoe rocked, but then went on—"Thirty-six as of his last birthday. Talent: Obliv-Obliviator."

Toes to hair, that was what Jo had told Renny, in a hushed whisper so Miles wouldn't overhear. Miles needed to be fully submerged in the lake for Jo to get her copy of his Talent. She hadn't explained any further.

As Renny pressed them into deeper water, Miles continued his shaky recitation. "Able to erase objects from the visual field of any pers—" He let out another *whelp!* when the canoe rocked again.

"It's okay," Renny assured him. It was hard to push out the words, caught as they were behind the lump of guilt in his throat. "It's only water. It can't hurt you." He swallowed the guilt down.

Miles nodded, but he didn't finish his Talent history. Instead, he stared at the water around them and flicked his fingers. Busy with his paddling, Renny was unable to stop him.

Flick-flick-flick-flick-flick!

The lake was quiet, except for the soft *slook!* of the paddle in the water. The occasional *hdup-hdup!* of a frog.

Renny could row back to shore right now, he thought, watching his brother. *Flick-flick-flick-flick-flick!* They could still make it to the arts-and-crafts cabin with enough time to join the Talent show rehearsal.

Except, if they did that, Renny wouldn't have anything real to rehearse.

It's only water, he told himself.

As Miles continued to flick his fingers—*flick-flick-flick-flick-flick!*—Renny stowed the paddle beneath his seat. Then, gripping the sides of the canoe, he took a deep breath and jerked, with all his might, to the right.

There was a fraction of a second when Renny thought the canoe would stay upright. And he was surprised to find that he was actually relieved. Renny didn't need a Talent. He'd been a disappointment his whole life, so why stop now?

He heard the splash before he realized the boat had tipped.

"*Miles!*" Renny shrieked, once he'd bobbed to the surface. He splashed in a frantic circle until he spotted his brother.

"*WATER!*" Miles shrieked, bobbing and flailing. His fingers flicked wildly. "*WATER! RENNY! WATER!*"

Flick-flick-flick-flick-flick!

"It's okay," Renny said, swimming the few strokes to Miles. The frigid water clutched at every inch of Renny's body, squeezing the breath out of him. "It's okay." Even though it wasn't. It wasn't at all. "Here. Grab on here." Renny tugged the overturned canoe toward them. Squeezed Miles's hands until he stopped his flicking. "It's only water." And then, from the shore, Renny heard Jo.

"Toes to hair, Renwick Fennelbridge!"

Miles's head, Renny realized, was still dry. In his life vest, Miles hadn't gone completely under.

"No *water!*" Miles shrieked. "*No—!*"

Renny grabbed hold of Miles's shoulders, and—swallowing down that lump of guilt—he pushed his brother under.

When Miles popped back above the surface, gasping and sputtering, Renny latched his brother's flicking fingers around the canoe's rope handles. "We need to kick, all right?" he said. Miles was fine. "I have a Caramel Crème bar back at the cabin. I've been saving it for you." Just fine. "Can you kick?"

Miles didn't kick. It was all Renny could do to keep his brother clinging to the canoe. By the time they reached the shore, Renny's legs were practically icicles, and his teeth were chattering. Renny grabbed Miles under his arms and walked him up the pebbly beach.

Flick-flick-flick-flick-flick!

Jo was grinning when they reached her. "Why, Renwick Fennelbridge," she said, and she looked proud. "I didn't think you had it in you."

For the first time, Renny wished he were a disappointment.

Jo tossed him a key. Silver, with a square top. The key to her office. "Help yourself to any jar you want," she said, her eyes fixed on the sun, which was just considering a dip toward the water.

Renny pressed the key into his palm, slicing at his skin. "Come on," he told Miles. "We'll change into some dry clothes."

———

Flick-flick-flick-flick-flick!

The whole way back to Cabin Eight, Renny swallowed and swallowed, but that lump in his throat simply wouldn't budge.

There were hundreds of memories coursing through the woods of Camp Atropos—big ones and small ones, heavy and light. Memories about building sand castles and practicing long division. Memories about trips to the eye doctor and visits to the shore with second cousins. One fellow even lost the memory of how to tie his own shoes. Some of the memories went whizzing on their way, eager to locate the perfect mind to settle into. Others took their time, floating along on the breeze with the birds. Miles had tugged many memories out of many minds, and most people didn't even notice their absence.

One memory—bitter like coffee and heavy like bricks—had been plucked from the mind of Liliana Vera, while she was standing outside the arts-and-crafts cabin. Lily didn't miss the coffee-flavored memory when it left. Truth be told, Lily might have been happiest if the memory had never encountered her again. But sometimes memories have a way of cropping up in the most unfortunate places.

The coffee-flavored memory crept along the dirt path, danced among the ants, and then slunk its way beneath the door to the kitchen, where a certain blond-haired someone was working on a batch of punch.

Lily

"LILY, WE'RE SUPPOSED TO BE REHEARSING!" ELLIE called from inside the arts-and-crafts cabin. "It's on the schedule!"

Lily wound the length of yarn around her thumb. There was an itch below her ear, but as hard as she scratched, she couldn't seem to reach it.

"No one else is even here," Lily replied through the window. Miles and Renny had branched off somewhere on their way over. "Where's Chuck?"

"I haven't seen her since free swim," Ellie said, and Lily could practically hear her frown.

Lily looked left, then right. The coast was clear.

"Tomorrow's dress rehearsal, you know," Ellie called through the window. "Are you going to practice with me or not?"

It was now or never.

"Lily?"

But Lily was already kicking up dirt on the path to the lodge. When she reached Jo's office window, Lily focused her thoughts at the bridge of her nose, twisted the latch, and *cre-eeak!*ed the window open.

Hundreds and hundreds of jars, lined up on the shelf. All of them with brightly colored bracelets at the bottom, holding Mimicked Talents.

Lily shifted her focus and concentrated hard.

Together, the jars began to rise.

Up.

Up.

Up.

Straight off the shelves, into the air.

Everyone was busy rehearsing for the Talent show, so they didn't see it: the jars, floating out the window, clanking against one another. Lily, her thoughts focused, *focused*, at the bridge of her nose, walking backward down the path. The jars, clattering in the dirt as they followed, past the archery ring, through the trees, to the center of the camp, like a long row of glass ducklings.

No one saw as the jars wove their way to the Camp Atropos

fire circle, through the spiral of logs, through the ring of rocks, under the heap of chopped wood, down deep into the ash at the heart of the fire pit where, once the fire was set that evening, the jars, along with the Talent bracelets inside them, would be sure to melt into nothingness.

Every last jar.

Well, every last jar save two.

As Fate would have it, two jars remained in Jo's office.

One was the jar that had wedged itself under the filing cabinet the week before, its label firmly affixed, with a green Talent bracelet settled at the bottom.

The second, with a yellow bracelet inside, was one that, as Fate would have it, Lily had failed to carry off with the others. That jar sat all alone on the very bottom shelf, and the ink on its label was so smeared that it was nearly impossible to read.

15

Renny

MILES HAD BEEN ACTING STRANGE—STRANGER THAN usual—since the lake.

"We're supposed to be at the campfire," Renny told him, when he'd finished rubbing the lake water out of Miles's hair. "That's what it says on the schedule. Friday Night Campfire. Then the slumber party, in the lodge." Out the window, Renny watched orange sparks light up the darkening sky as campers streamed to the fire circle at the center of the camp.

But Miles seemed completely uninterested in schedules. "You have to get a jar from Jo's office." He picked the key off the dresser beside their bunk and pressed it into Renny's hand. It felt cold. Sharp. "Jo said."

"We can do that later," Renny told him. Swallowing. "Right now we should go to the campfire."

"*You need to get a jar!*" Miles shouted suddenly. He began flicking his fingers. *Flick-flick-flick-flick-flick!*

Renny grabbed at his brother's hands. "Fine," he said, with as much calm as he could muster. "Fine, Miles, if that's what you want, we'll go, okay? But then the campfire."

"Then the campfire," Miles agreed.

There was a single jar sitting on the shelf in Jo's office, on the very edge of the very bottom row. Miles plucked it up and held it out to Renny, who was still gripping the silver key in the door lock.

"Here," Miles said. "This is yours now."

Renny examined the jar. A yellow Talent bracelet was coiled at the bottom, holding a Mimic of a real Talent. Even if that bracelet would only grant him a Talent for a single year, it was a million times better than the useless bracelet at his ankle, still murky with lake water, dyeing his sock a hazy blue-green. Renny squinted at the smeared ink on the jar's label, nearly impossible to read. COST, perhaps. Or COAT. All he had to do was slip the bracelet on.

"I don't need it," Renny told his brother, pressing his fingers tighter around the key in the lock. "Put it back. Let's go."

Miles didn't put the jar back. "But it's *yours*," he insisted.

"Jo said for you to have it, because you pushed me under the water."

Renny was certain then that no amount of swallowing would ever dislodge the lump of guilt in his throat. "You heard that?" he said. He searched Miles's eyes for anger. Disappointment. Betrayal. Something.

But Miles just looked like Miles.

"It's yours," Miles told him again. "You earned it."

Renny took the jar. Examined the yellow bracelet inside. "I . . ." He could apologize. Put the jar back on the shelf and lock the office door.

Renny slid the jar into his pocket.

"You're okay," he told Miles. "Right? It was only water."

"Only water," Miles replied.

Renny swallowed again.

Lily

Lily had planned on sitting beside Max during the campfire. (There'd be no room on the log, she hoped, for Hannah.) As the sky grew darker and the fire grew warmer, everyone would sing songs from atop their logs, and Jo's jars of bracelets with their Mimicked Talents would melt silently away. And Lily would turn to Max and say, *I stopped a criminal.* Max's eyes would grow wide with amazement. *You did?* he'd say. *Wow. That's WAY better than making punch.*

That's what Lily had planned.

But when she reached the fork in the path—left for the fire circle, right for the lake—Lily noticed the frog. Even in the dim light of the setting sun, the frog was bright green, and white at the throat, with bulby pads at the ends of his toes. He was squatting directly in front of her, tilting his froggy head as though he wanted to tell her something. Lily glanced left, then right. No one else seemed to see him.

Hdup-hdup! went the frog. And then he shifted to the right, and hopped away from the fire circle, toward the cold, quiet waters of Lake Atropos.

Later, Lily wouldn't be able to say precisely why she did it. Perhaps it was Fate. Perhaps it was simple curiosity. Whatever the reason, Liliana Vera followed the frog.

Jo

EVERY EVENING FOR THE PAST FIVE YEARS, JO HAD waited on the southernmost bank of Lake Atropos, watching the tide lap at the shore. Most nights she carried baskets with her, to haul away her loot. Tonight she brought nothing but Grandma Esther's harmonica. The sky blazed fiery orange nearest the water, edging into watermelon pink farther up, then, at its height, a deep blackberry, and lily pads dotted the shore.

Precisely at the moment when the sun sank fully below the horizon, a familiar, beautiful sound rang through the darkness. It always began low and slow, growing sharper and more musical as the jars increased in number. Two jars, then ten, emerged from the water, pushing themselves up the pebbly shore.

Twenty jars, then dozens and dozens. Soon there were hundreds of them—all glass, sample-size, with the words *Darlington Peanut Butter* embossed on the bottom, and an orb of yellow-purple Talent at their center. Jo pulled out her harmonica and began to play. Searching.

> *Los golpes en la vida*
> *preparan nuestros corazones*
> *como el fuego forja al acero.*

Pearl, alabaster, porcelain, frost.

When she spotted it, Jo raced into the water, wading through jars glowing yellow-purple, snatching up the one she wanted. Jo clutched the jar to her chest, like a toddler might with a stuffed bear.

She didn't notice that she'd dropped her harmonica onto the pebbles.

Just in time. Jo had found her Talent for Recollecting just in time. In two short days, Jenny would arrive.

In two short days, all would be forgotten.

Jo unscrewed the lid of the jar and pressed it beneath her nose. The yellow-purple orb was dragged through her nostrils in one long *suuuuuuuuuck*. Immediately she felt the Talent seep into her bones.

Jo reached out for the nearest memory, testing her new

abilities. She found one easily, and wound it around her fingers. The memory tasted tart and smooth, like pineapple custard. She was picking out a puppy at the Fifty-Ninth Street shelter, she remembered. Pippet, that's what she'd named the dog.

Jo flicked the memory away—*flick-flick-flick-flick-flick!*—and let the empty jar smash to bits on the pebbles. The rest of the jars she left clattering in the lake behind her.

She left her harmonica as well.

Lily

LILY SAT AT THE EDGE OF THE PIER, HER FEET DANGLING over the water, wondering why the frog might have led her here. Far off in the woods, campers were singing, enjoying their campfire. Lily watched the sun sink lower, stretching its long rays across the lake. The sky blazed fiery orange nearest the water, edging into watermelon pink farther up, then, at its height, a deep blackberry, and lily pads dotted the shore.

"You think those Talents have melted yet?" Lily asked the frog beside her—even though she knew it was ridiculous to talk to a frog.

The creature's white throat was luminous against the darkening sky. *Hdup-hdup!* he replied. Then, precisely at the moment when the sun sank fully below the horizon, the frog leapt off the pier into the black below.

"Well, good-bye to you, too," Lily said, and she rose to join the others at the campfire.

She stopped when she heard the noise.

It was quiet at first, a whisper above the singing in the woods, but it grew steadily sharper and more musical.

Jars, Lily saw, searching the water. They lapped their way up the pebbly shore not fifty yards away. Hundreds and hundreds of them, glowing yellow-purple at the center. Talents, Lily was sure of it. She may have destroyed the jars in Jo's office, but here, somehow, were new ones, emerged from the lake, and *glowing*. The sight was delicious and frightening both at once, made all the more peculiar by a sudden familiar lullaby.

> *Los golpes en la vida*
> *preparan nuestros corazones*
> *como el fuego forja al acero.*

It was Jo, a shadow against the trees, playing the tune on her harmonica. Lily twisted the length of yarn around her thumb. An Artifact. Jo had an Artifact.

Lily was so focused on the glowing jars and the haunting music floating across the water, that it took her a moment to notice the footsteps on the pier behind her. Footsteps, and crutch steps, too.

"Max," she said, spinning around to find her brother. He was balanced on his good foot, using only one crutch, and he was holding a glass of something. A memory Hannah had concocted for him, most likely.

"When were you going to tell me about the accident?" Max asked.

Chuck

AS THE SUN CONCEALED ITSELF BEHIND THE TREES, ALL three hundred campers of Camp Atropos (well, all except two, but Chuck didn't know that) settled themselves onto the thick logs that spiraled the fire pit. Counselors fed the fire, scattering bits of blaze to the dark wind.

"There are two seats in the front," Ellie said, grabbing Chuck's hand. Ellie had found her when Chuck had gone to use the bathroom. Chuck had never felt so betrayed by her own bladder.

Chuck wrenched her hand free. "Can't I do something by myself for *once*?" she snapped.

There were plenty of sounds, all around them. The *thunk!* of wood onto the fire. The chattering of campers. The *hdup-hdup!* of a frog in the distance. But to Chuck, it seemed that her sister's silence swallowed up every noise in the woods.

"Sit wherever you want," Ellie said at last. And she left Chuck to take a seat beside Renny and Miles and Lily's stepsister, Hannah, in the front row.

Chuck found a seat in the back, at the very end of the log spiral. Del sat beside her, scratching a spot below one ear.

"Aren't you supposed to lead the campfire?" Chuck asked him. She thought that was one of his duties as head counselor.

Del scratched a little harder. "Normally, yes." *Scratch scratch scratch.* "I mean, I think so." He kicked his feet into the air, and Chuck noticed that his laces were untied, dangling to the dirt. "I'm feeling a bit fuzzy at the moment. Teagan said she'd take over."

As the frogs on the lake croaked their froggy songs, Teagan led the children of Camp Atropos in songs of their own. All the while, Chuck ran her fingers over the silver knot in her pocket—quirky and complicated and beautiful—watching the back of Ellie's head as the sky slowly swallowed her braids into darkness.

When the world around them was black as ink, Teagan declared, "This is our final song of the evening. So, in Camp Atropos tradition, let's all stand up and join hands."

Del reached his hand for Chuck's, and as soon as she took

hold, she felt it. The icy chill worked its way up Chuck's arm like a dip in a lake on a hot day. And it wasn't only Del's Talent she felt. Linked as she was with nearly every camper and counselor of Camp Atropos, Chuck felt them all. Racing up one arm and down another, the Talents came, surging through bodies they'd never inhabited before, cool when they neared her and warm as they pushed away.

As the campers' song filled the woods, Chuck wheedled some Talents forward and urged others back, until Del had Molly's Talent for time-telling, and Hannah could sense lies, and Miles could climb mountains with his bare hands. She tinkered with each and every Talent, savoring their varied textures. All except Ellie's. Chuck had spent enough time with Ellie's.

By the time the final breath had been drawn on the last note of the song, Chuck knew for certain what she was. She dropped Del's hand, hoisting one Kelly-green high-top onto the log behind her, then the other. She stood as tall as she could, and she shouted.

"Hey!" she hollered. "Hey! Everybody!"

The campers and counselors of Camp Atropos, just finishing their song, turned in unison to look at her. And Chuck saw Ellie's face then, her frown enhanced by the flickering fire, but she didn't care. She didn't. Chuck had something bubbling up inside her, and she needed to let it out.

"I!"

She belted each word.

"Am!"

She took her time with it.

"A!"

Savored each syllable.

"*Coax!*"

That was precisely when the first jar exploded.

Lily

"**Hannah told me about the accident,**" **Max said,**
making his way closer. His crutch pinched his shirt at the arm-
pit. He held out the glass of whatever it was. "Remind you of
anything?"

Lily scratched below one ear, confused by her brother's words.
But when she took the glass and drank a tentative sip, the memories came flooding back.

Coffee. The drink—and the memory—tasted of coffee.

"The bookshelf," she said softly. She remembered now, what
she'd done. She wished she hadn't.

Max's face was scrunched in anger. "Why didn't you tell me?"
he demanded. "Why'd you lie about it?"

Lily set the glass on the pier. "*Max*," she said, Hannah's beverage burning her throat.

She could apologize. Just two little words.

Instead, Lily said something else entirely. "You like her better than me."

"What?" Max's face scrunched even more, a rumpled shirt at the bottom of the clothes hamper. "Who?"

"Hannah!" Lily bellowed the name. She shook up everything inside her like a bottle of soda, and popped the lid. "All you care about is Hannah! I stopped a criminal, you know. I mean"—she glanced at the jars clattering against the shore, not fifty yards away—"I tried to. But isn't that better than making some stupid drinks? I put hundreds of jars of stolen Talents inside the campfire so they'd melt away."

"You did?" Max said. But he didn't sound impressed, the way Lily had imagined. "Why would you do *that*?"

Before Lily could respond, a burst of light—sudden, dazzling, alarming—shredded the sky above them, and a grand *ka-WRACK!* shook the woods. For a brief moment, everything was stunned into silence. The campers, the squirrels, the frogs, even the wind. And in that moment, Lily knew in her gut where the explosion had come from.

"The fire," she breathed. "The Talents in the fire."

Ka-WRACK!

Max jumped at the sound of another explosion, and watched,

dumbfounded, as another yellow-purple orb blazed a path through the darkness.

"*You* did that?" he asked.

Ka-WRACK! Ka-WRACK!

"I was trying to help," Lily said, her voice a whimper. *Ka-WRACK! Ka-WRACK!* "I was trying to help everybody."

There was shouting, from the woods. Terrified yelps.

"You didn't help at all!" Max hollered above the clamor of more and more explosions. The sky was awash with Talents now, dozens of yellow-purple sparks. It might have been beautiful, if not for the frightened shrieking from the campers at the fire. "You made everything worse!"

As the Talents skimmed across the water and the explosions continued, shouts growing louder and louder, Max stomped on his good foot back into the trees, leaving Lily alone on the pier.

"She's not your sister, Max!" Lily called after him. She wound the length of yarn around her thumb, *faster faster faster.* "I'm your sister!" But in the chaos, she was certain he didn't hear.

Renny

KA-WRACK!

When the first spark shot into the sky, Renny was so startled, he tripped over the log behind him, flat into the dirt.

Ka-WRACK! Ka-WRACK!

As orbs of yellow-purple were launched into the blackness around him, Renny pulled himself to his knees, his hands fidgeting wildly as a tiny scrap of something whistled past his nose. The object sizzled when it hit the dirt. A fiery shard of shattered glass.

"Miles!" Renny hollered, searching for his brother. All around him, campers were shrieking. Racing away with heavy footsteps. Hopping over logs. Thudding into one another, trying to avoid burning bits of glass. More and more sparks shot from the fire.

Ka-WRACK! Ka-WRACK!

Amid the chaos, Renny found Miles, on his belly in the dirt, his arm stretched under a log. He seemed to be grabbing for something.

"Come on, Miles," Renny shouted, tugging at his brother's arm. *Ka-WRACK!* "We have to get out of here."

But Miles wouldn't budge. "You lost it," he insisted, arm wedged under the log. "I have to get it for you."

Ka-WRACK!

"You don't have to get anything," Renny argued. *Ka-WRACK!* He dodged another glass shard. "We have to *go*."

When at last Miles dislodged whatever it was he'd been grabbing for, Renny was able to tug him to his feet.

"Here." Miles held the object out to Renny. It was the jar from Jo's office, with the yellow Talent bracelet inside. "You lost it." He pressed the jar into Renny's hand.

Ka-WRACK!

Renny yanked his brother away from the fire, pulling him toward the lodge, where the other campers and counselors were streaming.

All the while, his hand, with the jar inside it, twitched.

Lily

LILY STOOD ON THE ROUGH WOODEN PLANKS OF THE
pier, watching the Talents dance like fireflies across the water,
vanishing into the night.

You didn't help at all, Max had said. *You made everything
worse.*

Around and around she twisted the length of yarn at her
thumb. Lily had tried to destroy the jars from Jo's office, but
there were hundreds more already, clattering in the water
not fifty yards away. And the jars Lily *had* put in the fire . . .
The shrieks from the woods had died down, but Lily was
terrified to return to camp, to face the damage she knew
she'd caused.

Something caught Lily's eye. Among the pebbles and the clattering jars on the shore, Jo's harmonica glittered in the moonlight. Focusing her thoughts at the bridge of her nose, Lily lifted the instrument, one inch, then two. *Focused, focused*, she dragged it through the air, snatching it from the sky.

An Artifact, Lily thought, flipping it end over end in her palm. It was well used and well loved, silver, scuffed, and slightly dented at one end. Somehow Jo had used this instrument to Mimic campers' Talents. Somehow she had used it to draw jars out of the water.

Lily knew quite a bit about Artifacts, more than most people, and she knew they could be used to do great things. But they could be dangerous, too.

I think you're more dangerous than she is.

That's what Renny had told Lily, just that afternoon.

Around and around went the yarn at her thumb.

Pickles.

Just when the length of yarn threatened to snap in two from the twisting, a new memory wiggled its way into Lily's mind. A very recent one, from someone at the campfire. The memory tasted tangy, like pickles.

She was watching Chuck, she remembered. Chuck had hauled herself up on a log to declare something.

A Coax, Lily remembered. That was what Chuck had said.

Lily worked the pickle-flavored memory around in her mind, until she was absolutely certain of it.

Around and around and around.

When the sky was black as a fresh chalkboard, no Talents in sight, Lily let her gaze settle on the harmonica. Perhaps she had a way to fix things once and for all.

Chuck

"You got incredibly lucky there, child," Nurse Bonnie said, dabbing at Chuck's forehead with some sort of chilly goop. Chuck flinched as it stung her skin. "I saw the sight from here. It was terrifying." Immediately after the explosion, the infirmary had been packed with campers, crowding the beds, perched on the dressers, smushed into corners, all of them needing Nurse Bonnie's attention. Most had suffered only minor scrapes and bruises. After administering a salve or three, Nurse Bonnie shuttled the children off to the lodge for the slumber party. Now, hours later, only Chuck remained. "I've never had so many campers injured all at once. And you got it worse than anyone."

"I'm fine," Chuck replied, although she didn't feel entirely fine. As it turned out, standing atop a log was precisely the worst place to be in an explosion.

"Two inches lower, and this one would've taken your eye," Nurse Bonnie told her. "The salve will heal your burns in a few hours, but you're staying here overnight. No slumber party for you."

Chuck found she wasn't upset about that one. She hadn't much been looking forward to watching a movie squeezed up against Ellie anyway. At least in the infirmary, Chuck could avoid her sister's disapproving frown.

"Ellie!" Nurse Bonnie said as Chuck's twin stepped through the curtains. The nurse took the girl in, head to toe. "No cuts or bruises. Don't tell me—you've lost a memory. We've had a rash of forgetfulness this session. Molly was just in here, all worked up about forgetting the name of her puppy. And Jason couldn't even recall tonight's campfire." Nurse Bonnie dabbed another smear of goop on Chuck's forehead. "I would have Hannah whip you up one of her drinks, but I'm afraid her Talent wound up with someone else, and I haven't had a moment to figure out who."

"No, it's not a"—Ellie wouldn't even *look* at Chuck—"a memory. Del needs Chuck in the lodge. He said she has to come and Eke everyone's Talent's back right away."

"It's not Eking," Chuck said. "I'm a Coax." But she'd hardly gotten the words out before Ellie snapped her eyes up. Her frown was so furious that Chuck wished she'd go back to staring at the floor.

Nurse Bonnie set the salve on the shelf behind her with a soft *clack*. "You tell Del," she said, "that my patient needs to rest. She can swap Talents in the morning."

"But everyone has the wrong ones!" Ellie cried. "No one knows what to do!"

"I'm sure you'll all survive the evening. Now, if you don't mind . . ." She plopped a pair of folded camp pajamas on the chair beside the bed. The toes of Chuck's Kelly-green high-tops poked out underneath. "Chuck, I'll run to your cabin to get your toothbrush. You girls can visit for a moment, but our patient needs her *rest*." She fixed a stern look on Ellie when she said that last word.

When Nurse Bonnie left the room, Ellie didn't sit beside Chuck above the blankets, or put a hand to Chuck's forehead, or ask if she was okay. Instead, she stared at the floor and said, "You switched all the Talents."

Chuck must have been holding the sigh inside her for ages, because when she let it out, it was the biggest thing in the room. "I know you want me to be a Frog Twin," she told her sister. "But I can't. I'm *not*."

"You switched all the Talents," Ellie repeated, to the floor and not to Chuck, "except mine."

———

At that, Chuck snorted. "The person who got it would've been *so mad*. I mean, seriously, Ellie. Identifying frogs is *so boring*."

The look on her sister's face then—sad and small and stricken—was worse than any frown. Chuck could apologize. Just two little words.

She didn't.

Instead she said nothing.

"A lot of people are really mad at you, you know," Ellie said at last, "for Eking their Talents without even asking."

"It's not *Eking*," Chuck said again. "It's *Coaxing*. It's really unique, Ellie."

"Well," Ellie replied, "at least only one of us has to be boring."

And with that, she left the infirmary.

As she changed into the pajamas Nurse Bonnie had left, Chuck clenched and unclenched her hand, trying to push away the memory of that look on Ellie's face, sad and small and stricken. But it was stuck in Chuck's mind like peanut butter on crackers.

Chuck flopped back on her pillow, ready for a long night's sleep.

It wasn't a full second before the next unexpected visitor burst into the infirmary.

Lily

"ARE YOU *SURE* YOU WANT TO DO THIS?" CHUCK ASKED, wrinkling her nose at the harmonica. Lily nodded. They didn't have much time, she knew, before Nurse Bonnie returned.

She reached for Chuck's hand.

There was a cold pinch, like a snowflake, that started in Lily's chest, then worked its way down her arm. Lily saw Chuck breathe deep as the Talent reached her hand, clutched tight in Lily's. Moments later, the harmonica in Chuck's other hand let out a sudden, loud *waaaaah!* And, with the note, speckles of dust escaped, glinting against the moonlight as they wafted out the open window, the Artifact's former Talent dissipating into the night sky, lost forever.

Lily let her hand drop to the covers. "Try it," she told Chuck, darting her eyes to the harmonica.

Chuck lifted the instrument to her lips. "I don't know any real songs," she said, and then she began a shaky tune.

In-out-in-out.
In-out-in-out.

As Chuck played, she kept her gaze fixed on a container of salve on the shelf across the room. It rose into the air.

One inch.

Two.

Chuck stopped playing, and the container rattled to the shelf.

"It worked." Lily might have imagined it, but she felt lighter without her Pinnacle Talent. She floundered a bit when she shifted on the bed, the movement of her loose limbs newly unfamiliar. She wondered if this was how Evrim Boz's brother had felt, all those hundreds of years ago, when his Talent had been Coaxed into those scissors.

"And can you still . . . ?" Chuck asked.

Lily knew she didn't need to check, but she did, just in case. Focusing her thoughts at the bridge of her nose, she set her gaze on the harmonica in Chuck's lap. *Focused, focused . . .*

The instrument wouldn't budge.

"I could try to Coax it back to you," Chuck said. "If you want."

"There's no way to get my Talent back now," Lily replied, waving a hand at the harmonica. "Trust me. I know a lot about Artifacts."

"Oh." Chuck seemed worried.

"No. It's good. Don't you see? This helps everyone." And she even managed a smile. "I'd like to see Jo try to steal our Talents *now*."

As she made her way to the lodge for the slumber party, Lily wound the length of yarn around her thumb, imagining the look on Max's face when she told him what she'd done.

Renny

"**Do you want some punch?**" **Renny asked his** brother as they rolled their sleeping bags onto the lodge floor. Miles had picked the spot by the door to the kitchen, which had the absolute worst view of the screen Del had set up for the movie. "Hannah made it this afternoon. I could get you some."

"No, thank you," Miles replied, crawling inside his sleeping bag.

Renny pressed his hands against his sides to stop them from fidgeting. Ever since the campfire, he couldn't manage to keep them still. "You sure you don't want to . . . climb the wall?" he joked. "Try out Nolan's Talent before you have to give it back?" Chuck had Coaxed new Talents to everyone, it seemed, at the campfire—everyone except Renny. Chuck hadn't given him anything.

(She had, in fact. But Renny didn't know that.)

"You could"—Renny's eyes swept the lodge, searching for a good punch line to his joke—"kiss the moose up there."

Miles zipped his bag around him. "I don't like kissing moose."

Renny settled himself into his own sleeping bag, not even bothering to change into his pajamas. When he was sure Miles wasn't watching, he pulled the jar from his pocket, squinting at the smeared ink on the label. CODE, it could be. Or COOS.

"When are you going to put the bracelet on?"

Renny startled at his brother's voice.

"None of your business," he told Miles, his hands beginning to fidget again.

"If you put it on now," Miles said, "then you could use it at dress rehearsal tomorrow."

Renny searched his brother's face. "Are you mad at me?" he asked.

"You have to put the bracelet on," Miles said, his voice as flat as if he were reciting Talent history. "You earned it."

No matter how hard Renny pressed his hands into his sides, they still kept fidgeting. "It was only *water*," he whispered to Miles, when the lodge lights had dimmed and the movie had started. "You can't be mad at me, because it was only water."

Spinach.

The memory hit Renny hard, and it tasted rancid, like spin-ach that had sat too long in the refrigerator.

He'd been young, Renny remembered, scratching the turned-spinach memory. A toddler. He'd wandered through a gate, toward a sparkling swimming pool.

Sputtering-and-gagging-and-coughing-and-screaming. Renny pressed his hands hard against his sides as he tasted the rest of the memory. Willed his heart to slow in his chest.

"Why didn't you ever tell me you almost drowned?" he asked his brother. It was Miles's memory he'd gotten, Renny was sure of it. "Why didn't you tell me that's why you're afraid of water?"

Miles didn't answer. In the darkness, Renny watched his brother's sleeping bag rise and fall with breath, and he rolled the turned-spinach memory over and over. *Scratch scratch.* He pressed his hands into his sides to stop them from fidgeting.

It wasn't until he was on the edge of sleep that it occurred to Renny to wonder how Miles had given him his memory, after his Recollecting Talent had been Coaxed to someone else.

Deep in the night, Renny awoke. The lodge was still except for the gentle breathing of sleeping campers. The jar in Renny's pocket poked his hip. All was exactly as it had been when Renny had drifted off to sleep. All but Miles.

Miles was gone.

Chuck

CHUCK PULLED A PILLOW OVER HER HEAD, SHIFTING TO face the wall. She was finding it difficult to sleep, with the harmonica on the bedside table gleaming in the moonlight.

Ellie had said that everyone was mad at her for Coaxing their Talents. But Ellie was mad at Chuck for *not* Coaxing hers. And then there was Lily, who'd practically begged to have her Talent trapped away forever.

Chuck smushed the pillow harder against her head. As soon as the sun rose, she decided, she was going for a good, long swim. A dip in the lake ought to make her feel better.

Renny's Orange Cream Smoothie

— a drink reminiscent of quiet nights on empty piers —

FOR THE SMOOTHIE:
- 1 cup fresh-squeezed or store-bought orange juice
- 1 tsp freshly grated orange zest—less than 1 orange
  (optional)
- 1 large banana, frozen (see Note)
- ½ cup plain yogurt
- 1 tsp vanilla

Combine all ingredients in a blender or food processor, and blend until smooth. Serve immediately.

[Serves 1]

NOTE: To freeze bananas, peel them, then store them inside a plastic ziplock bag in the freezer for several hours or overnight. This is a great use for overripe or mushy bananas.

Renny

RENNY STOOD ON THE PIER ABOVE LAKE ATROPOS, pressing his hands into his sides to stop the fidgeting. It hadn't been difficult to slip out the back kitchen door of the lodge. Judging from the Caramel Crème wrappers littering the kitchen floor, it was precisely how Miles had escaped, too.

Renny reached into his pocket and pulled out the jar from Jo's office. *Darlington Peanut Butter*, that's what was embossed on the bottom in curving letters. The yellow Talent bracelet shifted this way and that as Renny brought the jar to his nose, still unable to decipher the inky smear of letters on the label.

Renny stared down into the black water, lit only by the white globe of the moon. Fifty yards away on the pebbly shore,

Renny heard a clattering noise, but he couldn't make out the source.

Miles had told him to put on the Talent bracelet. To claim the prize he'd earned. Renny should do it. He knew he should.

But he didn't.

Gripping the jar tight in his fidgeting hands, Renny pushed a thought to the very front of his mind. Miles may have lost his Talent for Recollecting at the campfire, but Renny knew *someone* had gotten it. And perhaps that someone would be able to pluck the memory out and pass it along to his brother, wherever he was.

You were never a disappointment to me, Renny thought. The memory was cool and thick and sweet, like orange juice. *Remember THIS.*

Renny flung the jar into the lake.

As Fate would have it, the small glass jar with the yellow bracelet that Renwick Fennelbridge hurled into Lake Atropos did not sink to the bottom entirely undisturbed. On its way down, the jar struck a large black stone.

The stone dislodged the jar's lid, and the bracelet settled itself among a patch of weeds, the treasure it had been holding in its woven threads seeping into the surrounding water.

Anyone who happened upon the scene—although of course no one would ever happen upon such a scene, not at the bottom of a lake—might have realized that the composition of the lake was shifting. It transformed quickly, before the sun edged its way back into the sky the next morning. Anyone who happened upon the scene might have said that it would be much too dangerous to swim in such compromised waters.

And anyone who happened upon the scene—well, anyone with a Talent for discerning smudged text—might just have been able to decipher the inky smear of letters written on the jar's lid.

COAX.

But, of course, no one saw.

Lily

LILY AWOKE WITH A START.

By the time she'd made her way to the lodge for the slumber party, Max and Hannah had already picked sleeping spots, and the only place left for Lily was half wedged between the refreshment table and a stack of chairs. Every time she'd tried to talk to her brother, he'd said he was exhausted—even though he was gulping down punch like a person with plenty of energy. So Lily hadn't gotten a chance to tell him about Coaxing her Talent into the harmonica.

Orange juice, Lily thought, rolling over the memory that had jerked her awake. *Cool and thick and sweet.* But just as she thought she'd snagged the memory, it fluttered away again, clearly not meant to stick to her.

Lily blinked once, then twice, then fell back to sleep.

Renny

MILES WASN'T IN THE EQUIPMENT SHED. HE WASN'T behind the archery targets. He wasn't at the camp store. (Although he'd been there, Renny could tell, because every last case of Caramel Crèmes was empty, and five bills poked out from underneath the register.)

Renny searched and searched, deep into the night, but his brother was nowhere to be found.

When Renny couldn't think of a single new place to look, he headed to Cabin Eight and curled up on Miles's empty mattress on the bottom bunk. Pressing his palms hard into his sides to stop the fidgeting, he fell asleep, his eyes wet with tears.

He'd never felt more like a disappointment.

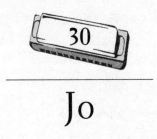

Jo

JO WOKE WITH A CRICK IN HER NECK, WRENCHING HER
head from her desk. She'd fallen asleep practicing her new
Talent—tugging memories from campers as they watched their
movie on the lodge floor. She'd wound the recollections around
her fingertips like cobwebs, sampling their varied flavors before
flicking them away.

As the first hints of morning shone their way through the
office window, Jo switched on her radio, hoping to clear the fog
from her mind. The station was just gearing up for a weekend
marathon of El Picaflor's most popular hits, in anticipation of
his newly extended tour dates.

Jo let the melancholy lullaby sweep her away. *One short day,* she told herself, allowing her chest to fill with hope. In one short day, Jenny would forget everything, and they'd once more be a family.

Los golpes en la vida
preparan nuestros corazones
como el fuego forja al acero.

"Come in!" Jo replied to the knock on the door. It was Del, carrying a large wicker basket. Behind him on the lodge floor, the campers still dozed in their sleeping bags. "Out with it," she said, noticing his sheepish grimace.

"I went to get the jars you asked for," Del said. He lifted the basket, seeming to mistake Jo's groggy blinking for confusion. "From the lake? Last night you said I had to get them first thing?"

Jo peered inside the basket, which contained fewer than ten jars. "Where are the rest of them?"

"Yeah. I sort of"—Del winced, as though anticipating a strike—"tripped? And most of the jars sort of . . . smashed?" He drew the basket before him like a shield. "These were the only ones that didn't break."

"Put them over there," she told Del, gesturing to the completely empty shelves behind her. That Fennelbridge boy had clearly taken all of her Talents last night, instead of the one she'd offered, but at the moment, Jo's happiness left little room for fury.

Del set the basket on the floor. "What are they for, if you don't mind my asking? Some kind of arts-and-crafts project, or . . . ?" He plucked up a jar, inspecting it. "And why were they in the lake?"

One short day. The smile that twitched itself onto Jo's face felt unfamiliar. She clanked three jars out of the basket. "You realize your shoes are untied," she said, by way of changing the subject.

"I still can't seem to do it," Del replied. "It's like the memory got lifted right out of my brain."

"I bet I can help with that," Jo said. She was feeling generous this morning. Nestling the last jar beside its brothers on the shelf, Jo began flicking her fingers—*flick-flick-flick-flick-flick!*— feeling around for a shoe-tying memory from one of the campers sleeping in the lodge. It should have been an easy enough thing to retrieve.

She found nothing.

"I am pretty exhausted," Jo said, mostly to herself.

Del nodded. "It's only six-oh-two and thirty-one seconds." He tapped the side of his head. "I got Molly's Talent for time-telling."

"Ah," Jo responded, only half listening.

"You're going to get Chuck to swap everything back first thing this morning, right? Because we have dress rehearsal today, and, well, in the mornings I like to freeze my coffee so the cream is a little slushy, and all Daria's doing with my Talent is making punch snowballs, so—"

Jo was still searching the lodge for a shoe-tying memory. Still coming up short. "Sorry?" she said.

"Is it too early to grab Chuck from the infirmary?" Del asked. "So she can swap our Talents back?"

"Sure," Jo said, attempting to blink herself awake. "Sure, go get Chuck."

No sooner had Del left the office than the phone on Jo's desk jerked to life. Jo snatched the receiver from its base.

"The Talents are wearing off," Caleb informed her, without so much as a hello.

"Caleb, I don't have time for this." Out of habit, Jo patted her sweater pocket and, horrified, discovered that Grandma Esther's harmonica wasn't there. "You can save your tricks." She tugged open the top drawer of her desk. Not there. "I'm not lowering my prices."

"This isn't a trick, Jo," Caleb replied. "I'm telling you this as your friend."

Jo yanked open the middle drawer. Nothing.

"It's been less than three weeks since I got that lock-picking Talent," Caleb went on. "And I can hardly unlock a door with a key."

The next drawer down. Nothing.

"I told myself I must be coming down with something,

because Danny put on his bracelet for the first time this past Thursday, and I swear, he could've spotted a lump of coal in a chimney at midnight—the Talent was that good. This morning? Jo, I'd be surprised if any new Talents stuck around longer than a few hours."

Jo slammed the last drawer closed. "No," she told Caleb. "I can't have lost it. I *need* it." But suddenly it wasn't the harmonica she was worried about.

"My clients are *angry*, Jo. They're practically sharpening their pitchforks. I'll do what I can so they don't come demanding their money back, but I can't buy any more Talents from you. I'm sorry."

Another knock on the door.

"I have to go." Jo hung up the phone. "*What?*" she sneered when she whipped the door open.

It was Del again, out of breath and clutching Grandma Esther's harmonica.

"Oh, thank *goodness*," Jo exclaimed, snatching the instrument from him. She flipped it end over end, savoring the familiar coolness of the steel, its sharp corners. "I think you were right, Del," she said. "We should have Chuck swap back the Talents as soon as possible." Someone in that lodge had gotten Miles Fennelbridge's Recollecting Talent. And perhaps Jo's copy of it had worn off—but why Mimic something when you could have the thing itself Coaxed right into you? "Have her come straight to my office as soon as she's up."

For the first time, Jo noticed that the grimace had returned to Del's face.

"Chuck wasn't in the infirmary," he told her. "Nurse Bonnie said she must've slipped out this morning."

The fury inside Jo boiled quickly. "Well then, what are you doing *here*?" she shouted. "Go *find* her! I want you back by noon on the dot with that girl!" Del went scurrying beneath the moose head and down the lodge steps. "On the *dot*, you hear me?" she called after him. "You think you can manage that, *time-teller*?"

With the last ounce of her rage, Jo whipped the radio from the wall, robbing Juan's song of its grand finale, and hurled it toward the window. But she missed her target. As the shelves collapsed on one another, the glass jars smashed to the floor, their useless Talents escaping in a whirl of dust.

One short day. Jenny would arrive in one short day.

Jo clutched her harmonica, taking stock of the scene on the lodge floor. Rows and rows of campers and counselors, snoring in their sleeping bags. Somewhere among them was a Talent for Recollecting. And fortunately, Jo possessed the exact tool to find it.

Jo pulled the harmonica to her lips and began to play, sweeping the notes across the room. Searching, searching . . .

> *Los golpes en la vida*
> *preparan nuestros cora—*

She saw no colors. Instead, Jo lifted hundreds of sleeping bags—with hundreds of snoring bodies inside—two feet into the air.

As Jo halted her song, the campers and counselors of Camp Atropos all smashed to the ground. The room was filled with the startled *"oh!"*s and *"ouch!"*s of children lurching into consciousness.

Jo examined the harmonica. It was Grandma Esther's, all right. Well used and well loved, silver, scuffed, and slightly dented at one end.

But it had been *altered* somehow.

"Campers!" Jo greeted the group, clapping her hands around the instrument. She foisted a smile onto her face. "How about we stretch our new Talent muscles, hmm?"

Jolene Mallory had been running a summer camp, in one form or another, for a long time. And if there was one thing she'd learned, it was that when things didn't turn out as expected, you needed to improvise.

Somewhere in the midst of that lodge was the very Talent Jo needed. (It wasn't, but Jo didn't know that yet.) So if *she* couldn't find it—Jo raised the harmonica to her lips once more—then she'd simply have the campers hunt for it themselves. Aiming her gaze at the moose head keeping guard above the double doors, Jo played her song once more. The animal plummeted down, sending a thunderous shiver across the lodge floor, blocking the room's main entrance and—more important—its exit.

"It's time for a little rehearsal," Jo announced.

In her haste, Jo forgot to ask Del about his mail run the previous evening.

In his, he failed to mention the letter currently stuffed in his back pocket.

Chuck

As the first rays of sunlight nudged their way between the trees' needles, Chuck strolled down the dirt path toward the sparkling waters of Lake Atropos. She kicked off her Kelly-green high-tops as soon as she reached the pier. Still in her infirmary pajamas, Chuck leapt for the water, dunking herself toes to hair. The water was both bone-chilling and delightful at once.

It didn't feel a bit, she would note later, as though the lake were Coaxing away every last stitch of her Talent.

Lily

"So you're not even talking to me now?" Lily grumbled at her brother. They were sitting on two of the folding chairs that had been set up in the lodge. On the stage before them, Jo was calling up campers and counselors one by one. "Try on your new Talent for size!" she'd tell them. "Show off what you can do!" Then, with help from the audience, the person would attempt to deduce whose Talent he'd been given, and Jo would make a notation on her clipboard and declare, "Lovely! Lovely! *Next!*"

This was clearly not a typical dress rehearsal. Jo was looking for something.

"I just can't believe you put your Talent in an Artifact," Max said, his arms across his chest. "Why would you *do* that? You know you can't ever get it back."

"I did it for *you!*" The words practically exploded out of her. "So you'd . . ."

So you'd like me again. That's what Lily had been about to say. *So you'd like me better than her.* But as soon as they met her lips, the words seemed silly, and she couldn't bring herself to push them out. "Jo's calling someone new," she said instead. And then she noticed who the someone was.

Hannah.

"I already know what Talent I got," Hannah announced, marching center stage. "It's Gracie's Talent for lie-detecting." From the front row, Gracie let out an excited cheer. "Someone say something, and I'll tell you if it's true or not."

"My favorite cheese is bleu!" cried a boy named Alfie.

"Lie!" Hannah shot back, with hardly a moment's debate.

"Yep!" Alfie seemed delighted to be caught in a fib. "My favorite's really ricotta."

"Don't you miss it?" Max said quietly. It took Lily a moment to realize he was speaking to her.

"Being a Pinnacle?" she asked. Around and around she twisted the yarn at her thumb. "Not really."

She missed it. It was like a hunger, almost, inside her. Aching. Gnawing.

"Not at all."

———

Up on the stage, Jo made a mark on her clipboard. "Amazing," she told Hannah. "Next!"

"This dress rehearsal stinks!" someone called from the audience. It was the large kid, Hal. "When are we going to switch our Talents back?" All through breakfast, which Chef Sheldon had served inside the lodge while Jo continued to help everyone "rehearse," Hal had complained loudly about receiving Liam's Aroma Talent.

"Soon enough," Jo told him. She flipped her harmonica end over end. Lily felt a pang in her chest every time she caught sight of the instrument. "Chuck needs a little more rest. In the meantime, shall we continue on, *hmmm*?"

"That's a lie," Hannah said. "About Ch—" But Jo was already ushering her down the stage steps.

Lily was certain that Jo was looking for a specific Talent. But what could she do with it, now that the Talent in her harmonica had been Coaxed aw—?

It was in that moment that Lily spied Chuck out the window, making her way across the mess deck toward the back kitchen door.

"*Fine*," Jo was saying to Teagan up on the stage. "The children can eat lunch. Is it really nearly noon already?" And while Teagan was herding campers into a line behind the kitchen window, Lily snuck past them and ducked out the back kitchen door. She met Chuck on the deck, and tugged her cabinmate beneath a table.

"You can't go in there," Lily hissed.

"What? Why?" Droplets of water beaded from Chuck's corn-rows onto the shoulders of her Camp Atropos T-shirt. "Nurse Bonnie said I was supposed to come as fast as I could. Am I in trouble?"

"Jo wants to use your Talent to steal someone else's," Lily told her. She was sure of it.

"Whose?"

"I don't know," Lily admitted. "But we have to get you out of here."

Before they could make their way down the steps, Lily spied a shadow of movement—Chef Sheldon, crossing the mess deck to the dirt below, letting the back kitchen door swing shut behind him. "This way." Lily jerked Chuck back across the deck to the kitchen door, and they slid inside unnoticed.

Through the frosted window that separated the kitchen from the lodge, Lily could make out silhouettes of campers waiting in line for Chef Sheldon's return. But the kitchen, at least, was empty.

And then the door was flung open.

"*There* you are!"

Lily's skin prickled with fright, until she saw who had entered the kitchen.

"Where have you *been*, Chuck?" Ellie said, hands on her hips. The door swung shut behind her. "Were you hiding from me again?"

"I wasn't *hiding*," Chuck growled. "I was swimming in the

lake." Something flitted through Lily's mind then. An orange-flavored memory, something about the lake. But she couldn't fully taste it. "How'd you even know I was in here?"

"The frog told me," Ellie replied.

That's when Lily noticed the frog squatting at Ellie's heel. He was the same one that had led her to the pier the night before. Bright green on top and white at the throat, with bulby pads at the ends of his toes.

Hdup-hdup! went the frog.

"You *cannot*," Chuck told her twin, "talk to frogs."

"I *can* talk to frogs," Ellie snapped back. "You can, too, Chuck, always could, whenever you Coaxed away my Talent. See?" And she reached out and grabbed Chuck's hand.

A look passed between the twins then. A look of confusion, maybe. Or concern.

"It . . .," Chuck said. "It's not . . . *working.*"

There were footsteps on the mess deck.

Lily grabbed Chuck with one hand and Ellie with the other, and dragged them both to the large metal cabinets under the sink. She swept aside the cleaning supplies as quickly as she could and drew them all inside.

Just before she closed the cabinet doors, the frog hopped inside with them.

Renny

WHEN RENNY WOKE ON MILES'S BUNK THAT AFTERNOON, hot and clammy, his fingers were still fidgeting. He pressed his palms into the mattress.

And then he noticed the sniffling.

Renny shot up so quickly that he smacked his head into the bunk above him.

"Renny?"

"Miles!" Renny shouted, hoisting himself onto the top bunk to join his brother.

Miles was coiled in a tight ball. He turned his face to Renny. "Hi," he said. And then he smiled, as though it were any normal summer afternoon.

"Hi," Renny answered, pulling his brother upright for a hug. Miles fell into his arms like a rag doll. "You were up here all night?"

"You did a nice thing for me," Miles said. "So I did a nice thing for you." He pointed to the shelf beside Renny's bed.

Renny laughed. "That must be every Caramel Crème bar the store had." The candy was stacked one on top of another on top of another.

"I want to eat one," Miles told him.

"Sure thing." Renny pulled two candy bars off the shelf, handing one to Miles. He hadn't realized how hungry he was until that moment. He couldn't believe Miles had been in their cabin the whole time, while he'd searched and worried. "But you *hate* top bunks," he told Miles, as though continuing a previous conversation. He hadn't even thought to check the top bunk. "How did—?" And then he realized. "You used Nolan's climbing Talent."

"Yeah." Ripping the candy bar wrapper apart with his teeth, Miles peered off the edge of the bunk, then jerked his body back to the wall. "Only Nolan didn't have a Talent for climbing back down."

"I'll help you get down," Renny told him. "You can hold my hand if you want."

Miles nodded in between chews.

The Caramel Crème bar was delicious. Silky caramel, smooth

chocolate. Renny had never actually tried one before, because Miles always got to them first. It was hard to believe that the company was going to stop making them soon.

"Maybe Mom and Dad should invest in these," Renny said as he chewed. "I think"—he let out a snort—"I think we should tell them *not* to invest in Camp Atropos." Miles didn't laugh at Renny's joke, but Miles never laughed at Renny's jokes. Sometimes it seemed like Miles was in a world of his own, and it didn't matter what Renny said to him at all.

But sometimes it did.

"Miles?"

Miles looked up, still chewing.

"I'm sorry," Renny told his brother.

Miles crumpled his empty wrapper. "I want another Caramel Crème bar," he replied.

Renny reached for the shelf. "I thought you said you got them for *me*," he teased. And then he blinked. "Why'd you say I did something nice?" Renny could think of plenty rotten things he'd done lately, but no nice ones. "I didn't do anything nice."

"You threw the Talent away for me," Miles replied, ripping open his second candy bar.

At first Renny didn't understand what Miles meant, because the orange-juice memory had been tugged from his mind. But then the tendrils that remained filled in the holes. "You got the memory," he said, amazed.

"Yep." Miles wolfed down his second Caramel Crème bar.

Renny settled back against the bunk's railing, his hands fidgeting ever so slightly as he shared a quiet moment with his brother.

He didn't think to wonder *why* it was so quiet.

Lily

IT WAS DARK IN THE CABINET. DARK AND STUFFY. LILY didn't know how long they hid. Three hours. Four. Outside in the lodge, the campers ate lunch. Chuck's stomach growled. The faintest sounds of Jo's rehearsal started up again, and Lily wiggled her toes inside her shoes. The frog, nearly black in the dim light that seeped between the cabinet doors, puffed silently in Ellie's palm, as though it understood it shouldn't make a peep.

Around and around Lily wound the yarn at her thumb.

As though being stuffed in a cabinet weren't terrible enough, Lily had to listen to Chef Sheldon's trusty assistant babbling as she helped prepare dinner.

"I just don't understand what Lily was thinking," Hannah said, "putting her Talent into an Artifact like that. And *lying*. Why would she lie about the accident? Max is really upset."

Just at the moment when Lily thought she couldn't stand another word, she heard the door to the mess deck creak open again.

"Where have *you* been?" Chef Sheldon asked, as someone stepped inside. "Jo's been going nuts, asking about you." Lily pressed Chuck and Ellie aside to peek between the cabinet doors.

"Jo said to be back by noon," Del replied. "I just went for a dip in the lake. It was so nice out, and . . . What?"

"It's almost six o'clock," Hannah told him.

Del rubbed the top of his head. "I must've lost track of time. Oh, goodness, I lost the letter, too, somewhere. Jo's gonna *kill* me."

"I thought you got Molly's Talent for time-telling," Chef Sheldon said, his voice laced with confusion.

That's when the orange-juice-flavored tendrils filled in the holes of Lily's memory.

Renny had thrown something in the lake last night. A jar, with a Talent bracelet inside.

Del had gone swimming, and now he couldn't tell time.

Chuck had gone swimming, and now . . .

In the dark of the cabinet, Lily reached out to Chuck, asking a question with a squeeze of her hand.

"It's not working," Chuck whispered. "I can't Coax anything."

"*The lake,*" Lily breathed. She dropped Chuck's hand.

When she was positive the coast was clear, Lily nudged open the cabinet door, then crawled out and closed it on the twins and the frog behind her. She tiptoed from the kitchen.

With everyone still "rehearsing"—although they were losing patience, Lily could tell by the decibel of little Alfie's whining— Lily reached the far end of the lodge undetected. She picked the phone off the wall outside Jo's office and dialed quickly.

"Dad!" Lily squeaked, the moment she heard his voice. When she realized she'd reached his voice mail, her heart sank. She twisted the length of yarn around her thumb. "*Dad,*" she said again, "you have to come get me and Max. I know you're traveling, but we need your help. It's important. The lake, something happened to the lake. This boy, Renny, dumped something in it, and now it's Coaxing away everyone's Talents. Dad, our camp director is danger— Hello? *Hello?*"

The line had gone dead.

With worried breaths, Lily turned around.

There, looming above her, with a single finger on the phone box, was none other than Jo Mallory. "Why, Liliana," she said, smiling down at her, "I really ought to thank you." Jo patted her front sweater pocket, where Lily knew the harmonica with her own Coaxed Talent lay inside. "You've just solved so many of my problems."

Jo

TIME WAS RUNNING OUT.

"That's it, there you go," Jo told the tiniest camper, Alfie, handing him a cup of punch. "Into the canoe. Del will help you. Lovely. Squeeze in, children!"

Del frowned at her as a girl named Sarah climbed in behind Alfie. "The safety warning says only three to a canoe," he said.

Jo ignored him, handing another boy, Max, a cup of punch. It was nearly impossible to be suspicious of a person, Jo figured, who handed you something delicious. After replacing the moose head on the lodge wall, Jo had floated every pitcher outside behind her with the help of a little harmonica music. "Max, your crutches can go under the seat right there. Del, help Max, will you?" When Del had pushed that canoe out into the water, Jo turned to the next camper in line. "Hannah! You can sit up front. This punch is delicious, by the way. Thank you!"

"You're welcome," Hannah said, her long blond hair swishing behind her. "Can I get a life jacket, please? I can't—"

"That's it, watch your step."

"Are you sure we need to do this drill *now*?" Del went on, when Hannah's canoe was safely afloat. Far out on the lake, Lily kept standing to holler at the others, but the splashing of paddles drowned out her words. "It's so late," Del continued, "and the kids never got an actual dress rehearsal in. The Talent show's tomorrow, yesterday was pretty rough on everyone, and the sun's going to set any—"

Jo's look silenced him for good. "Have some punch, Tessa. There you go, in the canoe. I *love* your necklace, by the way. Did you make that in arts and crafts?"

Time was running out.

With Chuck missing and no inkling where the Recollecting Talent might have landed, Jo's only hope was that Lily had been right about the lake Coaxing Talents. If it was true, then come sunset, Jo suspected there would be a whole new stash of jars washing in with the tide. Only this time, the jars wouldn't hold Mimics of Talents. This time they'd hold the Talents themselves.

———

It was only a hunch. A single shred of hope. But with Jenny arriving in one short day, it was the last shred Jo had.

The sun was nearly touching the water when Jo pushed the final canoe into the lake, the water bursting with every camper and counselor Camp Atropos had.

(Well, every camper except four, but Jo didn't know that.)

"Paddle, darlings!" Jo hollered, eyeing the distance between the sun and the water. "A little farther! Great job!" Toes to hair. They'd all need to be dunked toes to hair. "Alfie, why don't you let Wendy paddle? She's much faster." Lily kept rising in her canoe, a speck in the distance, to shout at the others. But Jo had ways of stopping such things.

"*Paddle, Lily!*" she instructed, and then she drew the harmonica to her lips, and played. Across the water, Jo heard the satisfying *slap!* as Lily's backside smacked the canoe seat.

Jo missed the Talent that Grandma Esther's harmonica had once granted her, but this new Talent was very useful.

"*Keep paddling!*"

The sky blazed fiery orange nearest the water, edging into watermelon pink farther up, then, at its height, a deep blackberry. Jo knew that it was now or never. Her gaze fixed on the most distant canoe, Jo lifted the harmonica to her lips again.

Los golpes en la vida . . .

Splash!

The canoe flipped easily.

Preparan nuestros corazones . . .

Splash!
Another canoe tipped, pitching campers into the lake.

Como el fuego . . .

Splash!
And another.

Forja al acero . . .

Splash!
And another.
The black lake churned with splashing and shrieking and swimming.
And still Jo kept playing.

Chuck

CHUCK KICKED THE CABINET OPEN WITH HER KELLY-green high-tops, scrambling into the brightness. Ellie and the frog climbed out behind her.

In the distance, Chuck heard a splash. Then another, and another. Through the window, Chuck saw dozens of canoes tipping into the water, with more capsizing every second. And orchestrating everything—a dot on the shore—was Jo, playing the harmonica with Lily's Talent inside.

The Talent that Chuck had Coaxed inside.

What can I do? Chuck wondered. And, perhaps out of habit, she grabbed Ellie's hand.

She felt nothing. No icy spark.

That's when Ellie said softly, "I still have my Talent."

Chuck wanted to roll her eyes. She wanted to sigh and say, *Identifying* frogs? *Ellie, please.*

But she didn't. Instead she puffed up her chest, so the two little words she was about to say would have more force behind them.

"I'm sorry," Chuck told her sister. "I'm sorry I said you were boring, before."

Even though there was nothing to share, Ellie squeezed Chuck's hand. Chuck squeezed back.

Hdup-hdup! went the frog at their feet.

Ellie released Chuck's hand, squatting down to meet the frog. With her palms flat on the ground and her legs bent at sharp angles, she looked quite a bit like a frog herself.

"He says there's something in Jo's office that might help," Ellie said, tilting her head back to Chuck. "Under the"—*Hdup-hdup!* went the frog—"under the filing cabinet."

Chuck's eyeballs bulged. "*Ellie*," she said. "You really *can* talk to frogs."

Her sister pulled herself back up to her full height. "I told you," she replied.

Hdup-hdup! went the frog.

There was, in fact, something underneath the filing cabinet in Jo's office. Chuck found it easily, picking her way past the smashed shelves and the broken radio, the scattered shards of glass. She squirmed onto her belly and stretched her arm far under the cabinet, and there it was.

A jar. Sample-size, no larger than a Ping-Pong ball, with the words *Darlington Peanut Butter* embossed on the bottom. Nestled inside was a bracelet woven from green embroidery thread.

"The frog says to put the bracelet on," Ellie told Chuck. "Then"—*hdup-hdup!*—"then we'll both have a Talent. What? Chuck, what is it?"

Chuck held out the jar to Ellie, to show her the label, written in neat, blocky letters.

Ellie read it, then looked up at her sister. "Do you really think . . . ?"

Despite everything, Chuck laughed. "Looks like I'm a Frog Twin after all," she said, unscrewing the lid. FROGS was written on the label.

Chuck tied the bracelet to her wrist, letting the Talent seep into her bones. "I guess maybe I don't mind so much," she told her sister.

Hdup-hdup! went the frog.

Jo

As the last rays of sunshine clung to the lake, Jo tipped the final canoe. In that moment, she could have sworn that behind her, in the dark woods, she heard singing. A gorgeous voice, rich and deep. Lyrics to her wordless tune.

> *Los golpes en la vida*
> *preparan nuestros corazones*
> *como el fuego forja al acero.*

But when she turned to look, no one was there.

Precisely at the moment when the sun sank fully below the horizon, that's when the clattering began.

Jars, and jars, and jars.

They pushed themselves up the pebbly shore with the tide, each with an orb of yellow-purple illuminating its center, until Jo was buried to her ankles. Out in the black water, campers and counselors splashed and shrieked, but Jo was focused on only one thing.

With her harmonica at her lips again, Jo lifted a single jar into the air. Playing her song, she twisted open the lid and took a tentative sniff. When the Talent that wafted past her nose did not have an air of Recollecting, Jo let the jar smash to bits on the pebbles. The orb of yellow-purple drifted off across the water, to be lost forever in the wind. And Jo played another jar into the air.

Jo was busy, so she didn't notice him—the single figure in the water who was not swimming toward the shore. The single figure who was heading deeper into the lake, hoisting himself into an empty canoe, tugging splashing campers inside with him. The man had arrived moments before sunset, diving into the lake to do what he could to help.

He'd been in such a rush that he hadn't even thought to unclip his pocket watch.

Lily

EVEN BEFORE LILY'S BODY HIT THE WATER, SHE HAD only one thought in her head: *Max.* When she popped to the surface, the thought grew heavier, until she could barely breathe for thinking it.

Max.

She hadn't realized she was shouting until she heard her brother's reply.

"Lily! Over here!"

The relief filled Lily's lungs, so that she bobbed a little higher. Max was safe.

Lily sliced her way through the biting water, her arms nearly numb with cold. All around her, anxious campers fumbled for their overturned canoes. But Lily was focused on Max.

She needn't have worried. By the time she reached her brother, he was being pulled into a canoe with a crowd of other campers. The counselor who'd helped him held his paddle out for Lily, so that she might climb aboard as well. But when she reached for the paddle, she saw that the man was not a counselor.

"*Dad?*" she said, a summer's worth of tears welling up behind her eyes. "You came."

Her father's smile was warm in the cold chaos. Juan Vera may have been known the world over for his singing, but Lily had always been much more fond of that smile. "You needed me," he said. He reached the paddle out a little farther. "I knew there'd be no ease for my heartache if anything happened to you."

The tears wet Lily's cheeks then, and she didn't even try to stop them. Her father had come. When she'd needed him, he'd come.

Lily returned her attention to Max, who was scanning the water. "Are you okay?" she asked him. "Your cast . . ."

"I can't find Hannah," Max replied. "She can't swim."

The chill of the water clenched Lily's chest.

"Is that her?" their father asked, pointing.

Max nearly lunged from the canoe when he spotted her. "Hannah!" Their father caught him by the back of his shirt.

Out in the blackness, Hannah was splashing wildly, her head bobbing-then-sinking-then-surfacing.

Lily's father surveyed the swarm of canoes around them. "I don't think we can reach her." But Lily's thoughts were already focused at the bridge of her nose, her gaze fixed on Hannah, attempting to lift her from the water. And then Lily remembered that she'd lost her Talent.

No, she hadn't *lost* her Talent, not like everyone else in the lake.

Lily had given hers away.

"I can still help," Lily said, pushing off from the canoe, plunging deep into the icy lake. Kicking. Kicking. Kicking. She dodged canoes and campers, the cold seizing her skin. Lily raced for the one person she'd never thought she'd be racing for.

When she neared the spot where Hannah was thrashing, Lily snatched an overturned canoe. With one hand on the rope handle, she kicked the last few yards to Hannah and wrapped her free arm around her stepsister.

"I've got you." Lily felt Hannah's body relax, just a little, as she helped her grab hold of the canoe's edge. "Everything's okay."

That's when Lily turned to shore and realized that everything was very far from okay.

Hundreds of yellow-purple orbs of Talent were careening across the lake, lighting the black water like stars shooting through the sky. Jo was using the Pinnacle Talent—*Lily's* Talent, the one she'd given away like it was *nothing*—to smash every Talent out of its jar. These were no Mimics, Lily knew. These were real Talents. The Talents of every single camper and counselor at Camp Atropos, Coaxed out by the lake.

And they were about to disappear forever.

"What's happening?" Hannah asked, as they joined the crush of campers kicking for shore.

Lily decided the simplest answer was probably best. "I messed up," she told her stepsister. "I think I really messed up."

Hannah snorted. "At least now you're telling the truth," she said.

Renny

SALT WATER.

Sick from Caramel Crème bars, Renny and Miles had climbed down from their bunk and were heading across the shadowy path to the lodge to find the others when a new memory worked its way into Renny's mind. It was unpleasant, like a nose full of warm salt water.

"There's something happening at the lake," Renny said, his fingers fidgeting at his sides. Now that he was listening for it, he heard splashing. Shouting. Through the trees, he noticed orbs of yellow-purple illuminating the sky. "Maybe I can help."

Miles's face was near ghostly in the darkness.

"It's okay," Renny told him. "You go back to the cabin. I'll come get you as soon as I can."

Miles gripped Renny's hand tight. "No. I want to stay with you."

Renny glanced through the shadows to the lake.

And he made up his mind.

"Okay," Renny told his brother. "I don't have to go."

"No," Miles said again. "D-Don't let go of my hand." And then, his grip tight in Renny's, Miles took a step toward the black water.

Renny was so surprised he nearly tripped as Miles tugged him along.

"Howard Greenspan," Miles said, and it took Renny a moment to realize he was reciting Talent history. "Thirty-six as of his last birthday." He took another step into the trees, Renny at his side. "T-Talent . . ." One more step.

"Talent," Renny joined in. "Obliviator."

One step after another, the brothers made their way to the water.

Chuck

As Chuck and Ellie cut through the trees to the lake, the preposterous scene came fully into view. Campers churning in the water like carrots in a boiling stew, Jo's melancholy lullaby a bizarre accompaniment to the chaos. The orbs of Talent, glowing yellow-purple, that soared above it all, as Jo dashed jars on the shore.

Chuck turned to her sister to ask what they should do.

Hdup-hdup!

It wasn't a frog that made the noise.

It was *Ellie*.

In response to the call, the bright green frog with the white throat and the bulby pads at the ends of his toes leapt from the dirt, plopping directly onto Ellie's shoulder.

"You can talk to them, too," Ellie told Chuck, squeezing her hand.

Hdup-hdup! agreed the frog. Chuck understood the creature, she realized. If she strained. If she *wanted* to.

Forty-one Eastern spadefoot toads, seventeen male and twenty-four female. Burrowed into the dirt. Burying themselves under damp leaves.

Sixty spring peepers. Sleeping in trees.

Twelve mink frogs. Thirty-three leopard frogs. Eighteen common tree frogs. Thirty-seven pickerels.

Big frogs, little frogs.

Fat frogs, skinny frogs.

Green and brown and spotted and striped.

Chuck could talk to them all.

She threw back her head, releasing a vibratey song for the spotted pickerels.

Rut-rut-rut-a-rut-rut!

The pickerels emerged from the darkness—one, then another, then another—in response to her call. They hopped themselves into a line before her, froggy soldiers at attention.

Ellie called to the mink frogs.

Didda-didda-didda-did!

Chuck called to the leopard frogs.

Huuuuuuh-dut! Huuuuuuh-dut!

And when every last amphibian was assembled, Chuck and Ellie told them what to do.

———

Creeeee-creeeee!

First to respond were the spadefoot toads, speckled with orange dots. They leapt for the water, where flocks of Talents were escaping to the darkness. Hopping from canoe to canoe to lily pad to canoe, the creatures, one—*gulp!*—by one—*gulp!*—by one—*gulp!*—by one, snagged the yellow-purple orbs on the ends of their sticky tongues. The leopard frogs followed. Then the pickerels.

As fast as Jo smashed, the Frog Twins' hopping helpers snatched the Talents up, cradling them in their mouths, where they glowed yellow-purple through the thin-stretched skin of their froggy throats. After catching the Talents, they returned to the sisters on the shore, *puff-puff-puffing*. Waiting for Chuck and Ellie to tell them what to do next.

"Now what?" Ellie whispered to Chuck.

Chuck looked at the long row of glowing creatures before them. A little froggy army. "No idea," she admitted. But she knew that whatever they did next, she and Ellie would do it together.

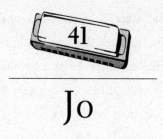

Jo

Jo DID NOT NOTICE THE FROGS. SHE WAS TOO BUSY lifting every jar from the lake. Unscrewing every lid. Smashing the unwanted jars to bits.

Como el fuego forja al acero . . .

The Talent Jo needed was not there.

As the rage welled in her chest—a rage so fierce Jo felt she needed to smash anything, *everything*, around her, just to squelch it—the last lingering notes of El Picaflor's song lifted an object from the water that Jo had not expected. An envelope. Soggy at the corner but, wedged as it had been between two lily pads, mostly dry throughout.

Jolene Mallory, it said on the front, in Jenny's loopy cursive. Jo stuffed her harmonica into her pocket and snatched the envelope from the air. Her heart thudded in her chest as she tore open the envelope and unfolded the letter she'd waited half a life to read.

> *Dear Jo,*
>   *I wish I could tell you that I'm coming, as*
> *you've asked me to.*

Jo hadn't realized that she'd sunk to the water, crouched in the shattered remnants of the jars. Frogs snatched yellow-purple Talents from the sky around her, the tide lapped at her bare legs, chilling and raw. And Jo forced herself to read on.

>   *I've read every letter you've ever written me,*
> *Jo. And I want to reconcile. I don't want to hold*
> *on to my anger any longer. I want to let it go. But*
> *you want me to forget what happened, and I know*
> *I can't.*
>   *In every letter you've ever written me, Jo,*
> *you've never once apologized. That's what I need.*
> *That's all I've ever needed.*
>   *I've waited, and I'll keep waiting, until you*
> *understand.*
>   *Ever your sister,*
>   *Jenny*

Frigid from the water, Jo at last looked up, blinking at the scene before her.

The glass.

The frogs.

The campers—her campers. Drenched and tired and scared, most likely.

It couldn't all be for nothing.

The rage welling in her chest fiercer than she'd ever felt it, Jo reached for Grandma Esther's harmonica in her pocket. But when she put the instrument to her lips, she found that it wasn't an instrument at all.

Grandma Esther's precious Artifact had been replaced, somehow, by a Caramel Crème bar.

Renny

RENWICK CHESTER ULYSSES FENNELBRIDGE MAY HAVE been born without a Talent, but there was one thing he'd always been very skilled at.

"That was *my* Caramel Crème bar," Miles said as Renny picked his way back across the pebbly shore, slipping the harmonica into his pocket. Miles was clearly anxious, this close to the water, but Renny was impressed with how well he was holding up.

Renny pressed his fidgeting hands to his sides, taking in the splashing and shrieking in the water. The frogs with their iridescent throats, lined up before Chuck and Ellie like troops on the shore.

"I wish there was some other way to help," he said.

"Fun fact," Miles said in response, his voice flat. "Only two people know about Renny Fennelbridge's Talent, and they have a brother bond."

Renny's head jerked up on his neck. "*Renny's* Talent?" he asked. But when he glanced down at his hands, he understood. He hadn't been *fidgeting* at all.

Flick-flick-flick-flick-flick!

That saltwater memory, Renny realized, that was one he himself had collected, wrapped around his fingers like a cobweb. He'd flicked Miles the memory from the pier, too.

"Can I get another Caramel Crème bar when you're done helping?" Miles asked.

Renny reached his mind out to the line of frogs, their throats glowing as they puffed. He found a memory easily, fresh like basil, and wrapped it around his fingers.

A spring peeper, swallowing a Talent for heat.

Renny reached his mind off into the water next, where chilly campers clutched at canoes. He found another memory, this one meaty like thick-cut steak. Hal Bernstein, first discovering that he could heat liquid between his two hands. Renny wrapped this new memory around his fingers, too. And then— *flick-flick-flick-flick-flick!*—he sent it to the frog.

The spring peeper tilted her head, and then, once she had fully digested the steak-flavored memory, she took a great leap toward Hal in the water.

The frogs on the shore, every last one of them, turned to Renny, their throats illuminated, as though waiting for the memories he could give to them.

Renny let his fingers flick.

Renny didn't notice Jo scooping up a canoe paddle. He didn't notice either that, in her rage, she began to whack her way toward the spring peeper leaping for Hal in the water. He didn't notice Miles, pulling the harmonica from his pocket as easily as Renny had pulled it from Jo's.

"I can play the harmonica," Miles said. "I learned last year in music class."

But Renny did notice when Miles began to play.

Lily

LILY AND HANNAH KICKED THEIR WAY THROUGH THE frigid water, bumping up against everyone else in the rush for the shore. At last they reached a spot where their feet touched the bottom, but with the press of boats and bodies, there was nowhere for them to go. There was no way to reach Lily's cabin-mates, and no way to stop Jo, who was whacking furiously at frogs with a canoe paddle.

The music that drifted across the water then was a shaky song, by an inexperienced musician, but Lily recognized it all the same.

> *Los golpes en la vida*
> *preparan nuestros corazones*
> *como el fuego forja al acero.*

It was Lily's father's song, the melody he'd made so famous that he'd earned the nickname El Picaflor. The Hummingbird. As renowned for his arresting voice as for his inability to stay in one place. The song was coming from Jo's harmonica. But it wasn't Jo who was playing.

At first, Lily thought that the water in the lake was being tugged from underneath somehow, like draining bathwater. And then she realized that it wasn't the water that was moving.

As Miles played her father's song, Lily rose higher and higher into the black sky. Water gushed from the tips of her shoes as she was pulled from the lake completely, and she let her arms fall, heavy at her sides. Soon she was floating, *flying*, above the splashing campers, being tugged through the air toward her cabinmates on the shore. The wind clung to Lily's wet clothes, and she shivered with cold.

She had never felt quite so alive.

Miles pulled the harmonica down from his lips just as Lily's feet thumped against the pebbles.

"Liliana Vera," he said. "Talent: Pinnacle." He held out the harmonica, shining silver in the moonlight.

Lily took the instrument, put it to her lips, and drew a tentative breath. It wasn't the way she'd used her Talent before—easy and focused and familiar. And Lily didn't know how to play any song. She could only draw in one note, then release another. *In* then *out*. *In* then *out*.

But it was so good to have her Talent back.

Lily played, focusing her thoughts on the frogs with the Talents in their throats, who were scattering this way and that to avoid Jo's rage. The frogs rose with the notes, higher and higher, away from Jo, through the moonlight, toward the campers in the water. Beside her, Renny flicked his fingers, and Chuck and Ellie *croak!*ed and *cree!*ed, and Miles filled them in on all the Talent history he knew. And together, the campers of Cabin Eight matched up frogs with campers. Lily watched as a spring peeper settled herself on the canoe in front of Hal Bernstein, and—*bur-RAAAAAAAAP!*—burped her yellow-purple orb of Talent directly in his face.

Hal gasped in surprise. And with that gasp—Lily watched it happen—he swallowed the glowing orb of yellow-purple Talent down.

Lily continued to play—*in* then *out, in* then *out*—and one by one, each frog found his way to the correct camper, and burped out a Talent. One by one, each camper swallowed the Talent down.

A frog burped at Chuck.

A frog burped at Max.

A frog burped at Hannah.

A frog burped at every person who had lost a Talent in the lake. (Well, all except one, but Lily didn't know that yet.)

When the final frog had burped out the final Talent, and the final camper had swallowed it down, Lily slipped the harmonica deep into her pocket and stepped into the water, where her father was paddling closer to shore. Lily helped him tug the canoe onto the rocks, and the campers scrambled out.

Max nearly stumbled, awkward on his cast. Then, rolling his shoulders as though testing out his rediscovered Talent, he balanced himself, hopping easily to shore. Lily led him to drier land. "I'm glad you're safe," she told him.

Max surveyed the scene around him. "I can't believe you did this," he said. And he sounded impressed.

"Well." Lily glanced at her Cabin Eight bunkmates. "I had some help."

Lily was so focused on the hug Max gave her then that she didn't notice Jo making her way toward them. But she needn't have worried.

"*Juan?*" Jo said. Her canoe paddle clanked to the ground. "What are you doing here? Did Jenny tell you to—?"

Lily squinted at her camp director, dripping with madness, and then at her father.

"*Joley?*" he said, his face dawning with recognition.

"You know each other?" Lily asked. But then she was struck by something even more troubling. "Dad, your pocket watch."

Lily's father's Artifact—the source of his great Talent and the object he'd protected obsessively since before Lily was born—hung from its chain at his waistband, rivulets of lake water escaping the hinge. He must have jumped into the water without thinking to remove it.

Horrified, Lily snatched the watch. "Maybe it can still . . ."

She popped open the face and twisted the watch key. But the gears would not budge.

It was Jo who said it. "You lost your Talent," she breathed. She sounded even more distraught than Lily.

Lily's father drew one arm around his daughter. With the other, he tugged Max closer, too. "Oh, Joley," he said. "I don't need Talent to be happy."

And Jo did something surprising then.

She began to cry.

"I'm sorry," she told Lily's father. "I wanted to erase things. But I'm sorry. I should have said so, long ago."

In most ways, Lily thought, Jolene Mallory was someone whose behavior she would never, ever want to copy. But there was one thing Jo had done that didn't seem so terrible.

"Max?" Lily said, leaning across her father to face her brother.

"Yeah?"

Lily reached for her thumb, where for so many weeks she'd twisted that swampy length of yarn. But the yarn wasn't there. She glanced down and found it draped across the toe of her sneaker. Just as she bent to pick it up, the frog that had been squatting beside her—bright green on top and white at the throat, with bulby pads at the ends of his toes—opened his froggy mouth, stretched out his pink tongue, and gulped the length of yarn down.

When he spit it out a moment later, the yarn had been twisted into the most intricate knot Lily had ever seen. She plucked it up.

As the frog disappeared into the thick of the trees, Lily turned the knot over in her palm, inspecting it. It was quirky and complicated and beautiful . . . and completely impossible to tie around a thumb.

"Yeah?" Max said again.

Lily slid the knot into her pocket beside the harmonica.

"I'm sorry," she told her brother.

It was time, she decided, to make some new memories.

Camp Atropos
Sunset Punch

—— a drink that combines an entire summer's worth of memories ——

FOR THE ORANGE LAYER:
  2 cups fresh-squeezed or store-bought orange juice

FOR THE WATERMELON LAYER:
  1 cup chopped watermelon, from 2 to 5 slices of watermelon
  ½ cup sugar
  4 cups cold water

FOR THE BLACKBERRY LAYER:
  1 cup (6 oz) fresh or thawed frozen blackberries
  4 cups ginger ale

FOR THE MINT LAYER:
  10 to 20 fresh mint leaves

FOR THE ASSEMBLY:
  approximately 10 cups ice

1. In a blender or food processor, blend the watermelon, sugar, and water until smooth. Carefully pour through a wire-mesh strainer into a pitcher or large bowl. Set aside.

2. Rinse the blender or food processor, as well as the strainer.

3. In the clean blender or food processor, blend the blackberries and ginger ale. Carefully pour through the clean wire-mesh strainer into a second pitcher or large bowl. (Do not combine it with the watermelon juice.) Set aside.

4. Fill 10 tall, clear glasses to the top with ice (see Note). Distribute the orange juice evenly among the glasses, filling each approximately one-quarter full.

5. Pouring very slowly, add the watermelon mixture to each glass, until the liquid reaches approximately two-thirds of the way up the side.

6. Pouring very slowly, add the blackberry mixture to each glass, filling to the top.

7. Garnish each glass with one or two mint leaves. Serve immediately.

[Serves 10]

NOTE: To achieve the sunset-like layering in this punch, it is important that the glasses be completely filled with ice. Pour each juice layer very slowly, letting the stream of liquid hit an ice cube before flowing into the glass. This punch is especially lovely served in jars, with drinking straws.

One Year Later . . .

Epilogue

CADY HAD NEVER IMAGINED THAT SHE'D HAD SO MUCH family just waiting to be discovered. And she'd never imagined that she'd discover them here, at Camp Atropos.

"I've never heard of a summer camp with an ice-skating rink," she said, strolling down the dirt path to the lodge. Through the trees, the icy sheet of Lake Atropos glittered, white and stunning, in the summer sun.

Cady's mother, linked arm in arm with Cady's stepfather-to-be, looked where her daughter was pointing. Jennifer had been linked with Juan for the better part of the past year, but Cady didn't mind. Once a mitten found its missing match, she figured, it most likely never wanted to lose it again.

"Del said he froze the lake to avoid any further shenanigans," Jennifer explained.

Cady's aunt Jo nodded. "Plus, now Camp Atropos is the only summer camp in the country to offer ice hockey."

Cady knew that her aunt Jo had once been the camp director, back when Camp Atropos was exclusively for Singular children, and before that, when it was a camp for Fair kids. Now that it was open to everybody, Jo had passed the responsibility of running things to her former head counselor, Del. "I need to clear my head for a while," she'd said. "Try to remember what's important." Aunt Jo liked to talk a lot about remembering.

"Cady!"

Poking their heads out from the double doors of the lodge were Cady's soon-to-be stepsiblings, Max and Lily, along with *their* stepsister, Hannah. When Cady had dreamed of a family all those years ago, she'd had no idea how quirky and complicated and beautiful families could be.

Together, Cady and the others entered the lodge, passing beneath the moose head keeping guard above, and found an empty row of seats to settle into. The room was bustling with campers and parents and siblings, preparing for the all-camp Talent show. Hannah and Max scurried off but returned quickly, Max balancing several cups of punch on his fingertips. "You have to try some," he told Cady.

From the seat beside her, Lily lifted her harmonica to her lips and began to play. Her song was shaky, but she'd improved considerably over the past year. As Lily played, a single cup of punch floated from Max's fingertips, through the air, bobbing before Cady's nose.

"The punch is really good this year," Lily said when Cady plucked the cup from the air. "Hannah's getting better and better."

Hannah beamed.

Cady examined the drink's layers—fiery orange nearest the bottom, edging into watermelon pink farther up, then, at its height, a deep blackberry. A mint leaf, like a lily pad, floated on top. She took a sip. The punch brought to mind Cady's best memories of summer—baking cakes on a breezy afternoon with her mother in the kitchen, humming beside her.

"Delicious," Cady said.

"Peanut butter's even better," came a voice from behind her.

Cady turned to discover two boys, one tall and broad, the other a bit skinnier, both with auburn hair and pasty white knees.

"This is Miles," Lily told her. "And his brother, Renny. They were in Cabin Eight last year, too."

"What are you doing for the Talent show?" Cady asked them. She knew that Renny had gotten his brother's Talent for a brief spell. But she also knew that Renny had insisted their friend Chuck Coax it back.

"Renny taught me how to take wallets from people's pockets," Miles said.

Renny's face flushed red. "We always put them back," he assured everyone.

Miles had already returned to his previous topic of conversation. "Peanut butter's better than punch," he said again. "But not as good as Caramel Crème bars." His fingers began to flick—*flick-flick-flick-flick-flick-flick!*—until Renny put a calming hand on his shoulder and the flicking died down. "Peanut butter candy bars would be better than anything."

Max was busy handing out cups. "But you can't put memories in peanut butter bars." He took a sip of punch, and by the time he'd swallowed, Cady could tell that he was thinking the exact thought she was. "Could you?"

"Peanut butter memory bars," Renny said, his eyes brightening. "Now, *that* sounds like an investment opportunity."

"It sounds like an adventure," Cady's mother piped up. And when Cady turned to look at her, Jennifer raised her eyebrows at her daughter.

Beside her, Lily flipped her harmonica end over end in her palm. "You'd need," she said, "some way to get the memories *into* the candy bars."

Cady's eyes landed on the two girls climbing to the stage for the first act of the evening—two girls Cady had met so many years ago, when they were toddlers at her mother's orphanage. Chuck and Ellie. The Frog Twins, they liked to call themselves.

As the sisters tapped their microphones and the audience

settled into an excited silence, Cady rolled an idea over in her mind. "Perhaps," she said—and the more she thought on it, the more delicious the idea seemed—"perhaps you might Coax the memories inside?"

Hdup-hdup! agreed a frog in the distance.

TURN THE PAGE FOR A LOOK
AT THE COMPANION TO

A Clatter
of Jars

Cady

Miss Mallory's Home for Lost Girls in Poughkeepsie, New York, was technically an orphanage, but there were hardly ever any orphans there. In fact, most days, if you peeked inside the window, you would see only one orphan, all by herself but hardly lonely, standing on her tiptoes at the kitchen counter, baking a cake.

Cadence, that was her name.

She was standing there now, Cady, deciding what to add to her bowl of batter. If you squinted through the window, you could just make her out from the chin up (Cady was barely a wisp of a thing). You'd see the shiny, crow-black hair that hung smooth as paper from the top of her head to the bottoms of her earlobes. And you'd see the petite—pixieish, Miss Mallory called them—features of her face. Tiny nose, tiny mouth, tiny ears. Cady's eyes, however, those were large in comparison to the rest of her. Large and dark and round, and set just so on a face the color of a leaf that has clung too long to its tree.

Flour, sugar, butter, eggs. Cady studied the bowl in front of her. She closed her eyes, digging into the furthest reaches of her brain to figure out what would be the perfect addition to her cake. At last her thick black lashes fluttered open. She had it.

Cinnamon. She would make a cinnamon cake.

No one knew exactly when Cady's Talent for baking had first emerged—just as no one knew exactly where she had come from. But one thing was certain: Cady was a Talented baker. She could bake anything, really. Pies. Muffins. Bread. Casseroles. Even the perfect pizza if she put her mind to it. But what Cady loved above all else was baking cakes. All she needed to do was to close her eyes, and she could imagine the absolutely perfect cake for any person, anywhere. A pinch more salt, a touch less cream. It was one hundred percent certain that the person she was baking for would never have tasted anything quite so heavenly in all his life. In fact, what the orphanage lacked in orphans it made up for in cake-baking trophies. Five first-place trophies from the Sunshine Bakers of America Annual Cake Bakeoff lined the front hall, one for every year that Cady had entered from the age of five, when her oven mitts swallowed her up to the elbows. No matter who entered the competition—professional bakers, famous chefs with exclusive restaurants—none of their Talents were able to match Cady's, not for five years running. Cady's cakes were never the most beautiful, or the most stunning. Last year not one but two bakers had crafted fifty-layer-high masterpieces of sugary wonder, studded with frosted stars and flowers and figurines. One even included a working chocolate fountain. Cady's single-layer pistachio sheet cake had looked pitiful in comparison. But nonetheless, it had been the judge's favorite, because Cady had baked it specifically for him.

This year's bakeoff would be held in just one short week in New York City, a two-hour drive away. Miss Mallory had already cleared space in the hallway for a sixth trophy.

The kitchen door squeaked open and in waltzed Miss Mallory, a polka-dot tablecloth folded in her arms. (Miss Mallory's perfect cake, as far as Cady was concerned, was just as scrumptious as she was—a nutty peach cake with cream cheese frosting.)

"What did you come up with?" Miss Mallory asked, crossing the room to peer into the cake bowl.

Cady found the cinnamon in the cabinet above her and popped off the lid. "Cinnamon," she replied, shaking the spice into the bowl. Cady had no need for measurements. "A cinnamon cake, three layers high."

Miss Mallory took a deep breath of pleasure. "And the frosting?"

Cady did not even need a moment to think. She *knew* the answer, sensed it the way other people could sense which way to walk home after a stroll in the woods. "Chocolate buttercream with a hint of spice," she replied.

"Perfect," Miss Mallory said. "Amy will love it." She snuck a finger out from under her tablecloth to poke a tiny glob from the bowl. "I hope this fog finally gives up," she said, sighing as the taste of the batter hit her tongue.

Cady had been so intent on her baking that she hadn't even noticed the haze. She peered out the window. Out on the lawn, the thick mist obscured all but the legs of the picnic table, and puddles speckled the steps to the porch.

It had been foggy the morning Cady was brought to Miss Mallory's, too. Cady had been much too young to remember it, but she'd heard the story so many times that the details were as real and comfortable as a pair of well-worn shoes. The damp smell of the dew outside. The mystery novel Miss Mallory had been reading when she heard the knock at the door. And most especially, Miss Mallory's surprise at the arrival.

"I'd never seen a baby so small," Miss Mallory always told her. "And with such a remarkable head of hair. There was a braid woven into it." Here Miss Mallory would trace the plaits across Cady's scalp, making Cady's skin tingle delightfully. "It was the most intricate braid I've ever seen, twisted in and about and around itself like a crown. Whoever gave you that braid was Talented indeed."

Miss Mallory snuck one more fingerful of batter from the bowl. "Perhaps we should move the party inside today," she suggested.

"But Adoption Day parties are *always* outside," Cady protested, slapping Miss Mallory's hand away playfully. There wasn't much consistency in the life of an orphan—new housemates coming and going like waves on a shore—but Adoption Day parties were always the same. Adoption Day parties took place outside, with presents and card games (it was difficult to play other sorts of games with so few people about) and a cake baked by Cady for the lucky little girl whose Adoption Day it was.

People sometimes suspected, when they learned how few orphans lived at Miss Mallory's Home for Lost Girls, that it must be a sorry excuse for an orphanage. But the truth was quite the opposite. The truth was that most of the orphans at Miss Mallory's found their perfect families astonishingly quickly. Miss Mallory had a Talent for matching orphans to families—she felt a tug, deep in her chest, she said, when she sensed that two people truly belonged together, and she just knew. Most of the little girls who came through the orphanage doors were matched within days of arriving, sometimes hours. Miss Mallory had famously matched one girl only seven minutes after she stepped off her train. They would send photos, those lucky little girls who had found their perfect families, and Miss Mallory would frame them and hang them in the front hallway, just above Cady's row of trophies. Smiling kids, beaming parents.

Cady had studied them carefully.

Cady was the only orphan at Miss Mallory's who had ever stayed for an extended period of time. Oh, Miss Mallory had tried to match her. Over the years Cady had been sent to live with no fewer than six families—loving, happy, wonderful families—but unlike with the other orphans, it had never quite worked out. Cady had always done her best to be the perfect daughter. She *yes, ma'am*ed and *no, sir*ed and ate all her vegetables and went to bed on time. But no fewer than six times, Miss Mallory had come to return Cady to the orphanage long before her one-week trial period was over. "I made a mistake," Miss Mallory always told her. "That wasn't your perfect family."

But Cady knew that Miss Mallory didn't make mistakes. Somehow, for some reason that Cady couldn't explain, the fault lay with her. And Cady vowed that if she ever got another chance, with another family, she would do whatever it took to make it work. One day she would have an Adoption Day party of her own. One day she would bake the perfect cake for herself.

"Maybe," Cady said slowly, glancing outside at the beautifully foggy morning, "maybe today's the day I'll meet my family." The very idea warmed her through just as much as the heat from the oven. She tugged an oven mitt onto each hand and opened the oven door, then set the cake pans on the center rack. "Maybe," she said again, "my real and true family will step right out of the fog."

The Owner

IT WAS AN UNUSUALLY FOGGY MORNING, SO MURKY THAT THE Owner of the Lost Luggage Emporium at 1 Argyle Road in Poughkeepsie, New York, could scarcely see the ground in front of him. But the Owner had very little use for ground these days.

He tapped his toes at the air, two inches above the soggy soil, as he finished affixing the sign to the Emporium's door.

ROOMS FOR RENT
CHEAP RATES!

The Owner (that's what they called him around town, ever since he'd opened up the Emporium, and it was how he'd come to think of himself, too) was not thrilled at the idea of renting out the building's empty upstairs bedrooms. But a hard look at his finances had finally convinced him that he had no other choice. Although his mother had amassed quite a fortune—an especially impressive feat for a woman with no Talent—it hadn't been enough to last him fifty-three years.

The telltale sound of tires starting down the long wooded stretch of Argyle Road sent the Owner floating back inside the building. It couldn't be Toby already—the dolt had only just left for the morning's luggage pickup an hour ago. The door slammed shut behind him with a crooked *wha-pop!* One more thing the Owner couldn't afford to fix.

The building had once been an architectural beauty, as famous for its two tall, round turrets as for the goods that were produced inside. Now, its white paint was peeling, its shutters were cracked, its windows were grimy with dust. As old and bleak as its owner, that's what Toby liked to say.

The Owner reached the circular wooden counter at the center of the main storeroom and lifted the hinged section to float inside, settling himself behind the register. A hastily hand-lettered green sign hung above the countertop, displaying the store's motto:

LOST LUGGAGE EMPORIUM
DISCOVER WHAT EVERYONE ELSE IS MISSING

"This is quite the setup you've got here," the customer called as he entered the store. Tendrils of fog curled their way in behind him before the door had a chance to close. *Wha-pop!* The customer jerked his head on his spindly neck, indicating the various sections of the store—the racks of clothing, the shelves of books, the electronics, the appliances, and, of course, the suitcases. "All this stuff really come from lost luggage?"

The Owner did not look up from his book. It was the latest Victoria Valence mystery, *Face Value*, and it really was quite good (although it wouldn't have mattered if it weren't). "Mmm," he replied.

"Nice Talent you got, too." The customer flicked a hand toward the Owner's legs, exposed beneath the hinged section of the countertop. "Floating, huh? Been a while since I saw a Talent like that."

The Owner stopped his toe-tapping just long enough to nudge a powder blue suitcase farther under the countertop. "It keeps the mud off my shoes," he muttered, turning a page in his book.

"Keeps the mud off your shoes!" The man hooted. "That's a riot." He shook his head, grinning like an imbecile. "Wish I had a Talent that good. All I got's whistling." And he puckered his lips and began to whistle a happy little ditty, right there in the store.

Finally he wandered off to peruse the merchandise.

He returned much too quickly for the Owner's taste, however (still whistling, unfortunately). "Ring me up!" the customer cried cheerfully, placing two worn leather bags and a winter jacket on the counter.

As the man dug for his wallet, the Owner, quietly and stealthily, slipped his right hand into his own pocket to find the small glass jar he always kept ready for a ripe opportunity. With practiced ease, he unscrewed the lid. Then he squeezed his hand into a fist. His palm grew icier and icier, until—*plunk!*—an almost imperceptible whisper of a noise escaped from the jar, and the Owner's feet dropped—*clonk!*—to the ground. The customer was too busy stuffing his items into a plastic bag to notice.

The Owner removed his hand from his pocket, just as he'd done so many times before, and stretched it across the counter. "I appreciate your business," the Owner told him. The customer suspected nothing. None of them ever suspected.

They shook.

"Ooh!" the customer cried suddenly. He rubbed his fingers. "Cold hands."

"Really?" The Owner's attention turned back to his novel. "Must be my poor circulation." And he didn't raise his eyes again until the customer reached the front door, where he (still not suspecting a thing) puckered his lips to whistle.

But, of course, all that came out was a weak cough.

When the sound of the man's car had at last receded down

the long stretch of Argyle Road, the Owner clasped and unclasped his icy fingers, the way a child might test out a toy he hadn't played with in some time.

Then, pursing together his lips, the Owner began to whistle.

There were eight bedrooms on the second floor of the Lost Luggage Emporium. On that foggy Friday morning, six of them were available for rent.

The Owner didn't know it then, but in just one short week, all eight rooms would be filled. Some would be occupied by people with great Talents, others would not. One would house a thief, a person in possession of an object worth millions of dollars. Several would be inhabited by liars. But every last person would have something in common.

In just one short week, every last one of them would have lost the thing they treasured most in the world.

It's
KIDS vs. *PARENTS*
in Lisa Graff's novel—

Keep reading for a sneak peek!

YOUR CLASS WRITES!

Pennsylvania's annual "Your Class Writes!" collective memoir contest is open now!

Tell us your class's story!

The contest is available to all Pennsylvania schoolchildren in grades 3–5

Winners will receive actual published copies of their book!

Submissions may be made in traditional narrative style or in "scrapbook" format

Deadline is Friday, June 9th

For more information about collective memoirs— as well as full rules—visit our website!

Mr. B— Here's our submission for the collective memoir contest. Everyone ~~contribbeted~~ contributed, but I did most of the writing. I tried to write it like a normal book, even though a lot of it is about me (that wasn't meant to be braggy, just the truth). Also, lots of people had notes about stuff (especially Squizzy), so I left those on so you could see them before we submit it.

Even if we don't win the contest, I think we did a pretty good job. It turns out we had a lot to write about!

—Winnie

P.S. We DID pass 5th grade, right??

(Please don't flunk us!!!!!)

1

"Treehouse 10" End Two-Week Siege

Wednesday, May 3rd
BY MARGARET WEINSNOGGLE

GLENBROOK—Parents around the world breathed sighs of relief this morning, as the second to last of the so-called Treehouse 10—all fifth-graders from local Tulip Street Elementary School—ended their 19-day standoff. Cheers could be heard from blocks away when the ninth child climbed down from the treehouse between the properties of Dr. Alexis Maraj and Dr. Varun Malladi, running to hug his tearful parents.

Everyone seemed relieved that the disagreement had at last come to a peaceful end.

Only one member of the Treehouse Ten still refuses to return to American soil. As of press time, Winifred Malladi-Maraj, the treehouse's original resident, remains inside, with no sign of when she might leave. Neither of Winifred's parents chose to comment.

Part I

How It All Started

Tulip Street Ten
(As Drawn by Winnie)

Pencils in his pocket (does he even use them??)

Test tube for experiment he's working on

Aayush Asad

Very curly hair →

Pet bird →

Pet turtle

Pet pug dog

Pet fish

Tabitha Borchers

Most acrobatic kid in class (if there's something, he'll climb it!)

Brogan Litz

Always telling jokes →

Ha Ha Ha!

Water balloons

Logan Litz

Winnie— Can you draw me with a lizard too? —Tabitha

Winnie, I don't think you should draw a lizard because Tabitha doesn't own one. This is supposed to be a <u>memoir</u>. Memoirs are <u>fact</u>. —Squizzy

But lizards are cool! I bet more people will read this book if there are lizards in it! —Tabitha

Tulip Street Elementary School

Where every child gets to bloom

360 South Tulip Street, Glenbrook, Pennsylvania 19066

A Note from Mr. Benetto

Fifth Grade Teacher, Room 5L

September 29th

Dr. Alexis Maraj
1 Circle Road
Glenbrook, PA 19066

Dr. Varun Malladi
2 Circle Road
Glenbrook, PA 19066

Dear Dr. Maraj and Dr. Malladi,

I'm writing in regards to your daughter, Winifred Malladi-Maraj. As I mentioned to each of you in our separate parent-teacher conferences after the first week of school, Winnie is smart, curious, and charming, and gets along well with the other students. Most days, however, Winnie is somewhat quiet. At first I believed this to simply be her nature. In my many years as a teacher, I have known many quiet students. And then I noticed something peculiar.

The minute Winnie walked through the door to Room 5L on the first Thursday of school, her face was brighter. All day she was more talkative, more eager to engage. It was as though someone had flipped a switch and brought this previously shy girl to radiant life. I thought that perhaps something amazing had happened the evening before to make her so cheerful. The next day, Winnie was back to her quiet self, and I thought no more of the situation . . . until the following Thursday, when Winnie was once again as carefree as ever. Something, clearly, had happened the evening before—something absolutely wonderful. The following day, the switch flipped back, and once again she withdrew.

I must admit that this morning, on our third Thursday together, I sat at my desk waiting to see which Winnie would walk through the door. And I am both delighted and puzzled to report that it was the happy Winnie—the girl full of sunshine. It's not bad, this weekly change in Winnie, but it is rather curious, and I was hoping the two of you might be able to shed some light on the situation. If there is indeed something on that occurs each Wednesday to make Winnie so delighted, perhaps it might be possible to bring whatever this thing is into her life every day.

I suppose my question to the both of you, then (and I don't mean to pry—understand I simply ask in the best interest of your daughter), is this:

What happens to Winnie on Wednesdays?

Yours sincerely,
Hector Benetto

The Last Day of Fourth Grade

a year before what happened happened

There are a lot of things you should probably know to understand why a bunch of kids decided to climb up a treehouse and not come down. But to really understand it, you'd have to go way back in time, and peek through the living room window of a girl named Winifred Malladi-Maraj, on her last day of fourth grade. Since time travel isn't possible, you'll just have to picture things. So picture this:

After walking home from school, Winnie stepped through the front door, with her backpack over her shoulder. Winnie's parents were sitting on the living room couch, with their hands in their laps. They were watching the front door, like they'd been waiting for their daughter for a long time.

Winnie pulled off her backpack and dropped it in the doorway. Buttons, who is the world's greatest cat, wove his way between Winnie's legs, like he knew she was about to need

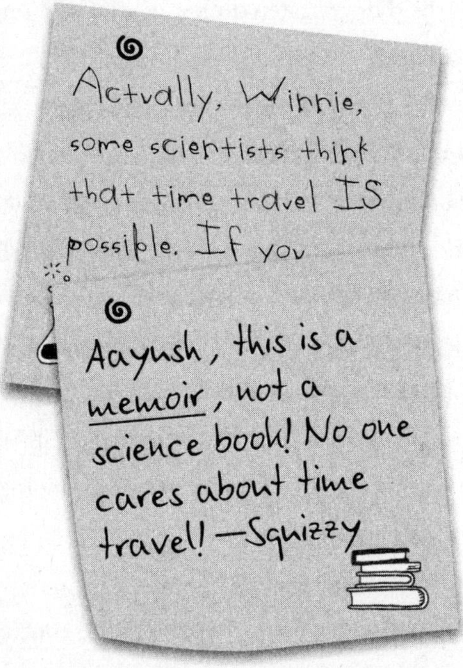

Actually, Winnie,
some scientists think
that time travel IS
possible. If you

Aayush, this is a
memoir, not a
science book! No one
cares about time
travel! —Squizzy

snuggling. "Mom?" Winnie said, squinting her eyes at her parents on the couch. "Dad?" She could tell right away that something weird was going on.

It's probably important to know that Winnie's parents have never been exactly *normal*. Like, instead of playing board games after dinner, the way some families did, Winnie's dad—a biologist—might sit her down for a slide show about his latest research on the beneficial properties of bat guano, which only made Winnie wish she'd never eaten dinner at all. Or Winnie's mom—a mathematician—might try to explain her current work on the Conway's thrackle conjecture, which only made Winnie wish she'd never grown ears.

(Once, Winnie made the mistake of asking if she and her parents could play Boggle after dinner, and afterward she'd had to sit through a two-hour presentation of all of her parents' many awards and grants—none of which, they informed Winnie, had been won playing *Boggle*—and a four-hour argument about whether or not Winnie's dad had more awards than Winnie's mom because there were simply more prizes for biologists than there were for mathematicians.)

(Winnie never asked about Boggle again.)

But finding her parents waiting for her on the couch together seemed *especially* weird to Winnie. Because, normally, Winnie's parents weren't even home when she got out of school. Normally, Winnie started her homework all by herself and then

Winnie, maybe write here that "guano" is another word for "poop"?
—Squizzy

Um, GROSS. We can't write "poop" in our memoir!
—Greta

heated water on the stove exactly at 5:55 p.m., so the pot would be boiling and ready to put pasta in as soon as they got home. (Winnie's parents were very precise about mealtimes.)

(They were very precise about a lot of stuff.)

Another weird thing Winnie noticed that afternoon was the way her parents were sitting. While she was standing in the doorway with Buttons weaving between her legs, she realized that she hadn't ever seen both of her parents on the same couch before. When they watched television or sat with guests, Winnie's mom usually squished herself against one couch arm, while her dad sat in the recliner on the far side of the room.

"What's going on?" Winnie asked. Even Buttons let out a confused *mew*?

"Come sit down," Winnie's mom replied, patting the couch cushion between herself and Winnie's dad.

"Yes," Winnie's dad agreed. (That was another weird thing, Winnie noticed. Her parents *never* agreed.) "Have a seat. We marked a spot for you."

And *that* was the weirdest thing of all. There was a tiny X of masking tape stuck to the center of the middle couch cushion. Her parents, Winnie realized as she stepped closer, had measured out a spot for her, so that she'd be sitting exactly evenly between them—not one millimeter closer to one than the other.

Pick up Lisa Graff's magic-packed novel.

Bernetta's summer couldn't be going any worse. First her ex-best friend frames her for starting a cheating ring in their private school that causes Bernetta to lose her scholarship for seventh grade. Even worse, Bernetta's parents don't believe she's innocent and forbid her from performing at her father's magic club. Now Bernetta must take immediate action if she hopes to raise $9,000 for tuition. But that's a near impossible task with only three months until school. Enter Gabe, a boy con artist who's willing to team up with Bernetta to raise the money. But only if she's willing to use her talent for magic to scheme her way to success.

How far would you go to get something
you really wanted?
Would you lick a lizard?
Wear a tutu to school?
Dye your hair green?

New kid Kansas Bloom (self-proclaimed King of Dares) and Media
Club maven Francine Halata face off in a crazy Dare War to deter-
mine the future news anchor for the fourth-grade media club (a gig
Francine has been dying to get forever). In a battle of wits and will-
power, Francine and Kansas become fast enemies . . . until they
discover that they have something surprising in common. And
somehow, that one little fact changes everything.

Albie has always been an almost.
He's almost good at tetherball.
He's almost smart enough
to pass his spelling test.
He almost makes his parents proud.

And now that Albie is starting a brand-new school for fifth grade, he's never felt more certain that almost simply isn't good enough. With everyone around him expecting him to be one thing or another, how is an almost like Albie ever supposed to figure out who he really wants to be?

Trent caused the accident.

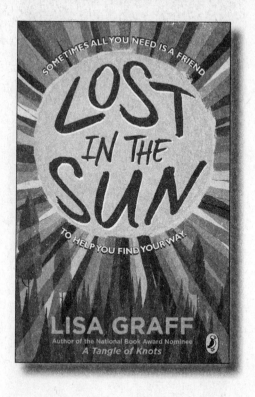

The accident that killed one of his teammates. But all he did was shoot a hockey puck. For Trent, middle school could be the chance at a fresh start. Maybe he'll blend in. Maybe all will be forgotten. Maybe he could even join the baseball team. But none of that seems likely. Then he meets Fallon Little—the girl with the mysterious scar across her face—and starts to realize that everyone has their secrets, and it might just be possible to start over after all.